When Bae Come Home
Home
A HOLIDAY STORY

Syfari Rhoades

ISBN: 978-1-7360783-1-0

DEDICATION

Deepest gratitude to my husband and children who've
shown tremendous patience and continued support
through this process.
This book is for everyone who has wished for a loved on
to return home for the holidays.

ACKNOWLEDGMENTS

Cover Design: Dar Albert, *Wicked Smart Designs*

Huge thanks to my editor and beta readers, with special thanks to beta reader, Marie Antwanette.

ADDITIONAL WORK BY SYFARI RHOADES

Entangled – Caught Up In His Web available at
https://www.amazon.com/dp/B08MT9G2WT

Join the *Rhoades Readers* mailing list at
www.rhoadeshousepublishing.com and be the first to be
notified of new releases, news, and contests!

Thank you for reading this novella!

Syfari Rhoades

WISHING FOR A MIRACLE

1

The aching enveloped her from the heels of her feet to the spine of her back. It hurt, bad. But this was a good hurt. She felt pride after putting in an honest, hard day's work. She didn't need anyone to push her; she was self–motivated. That's how she landed the Assistant Manager position at *Daylight Dreams* in the downtown area of Detroit. She worked there for the past three years, having worked her way up from a Sales Assistant.

Daylight Dreams was a small boutique store within a bus ride and walking distance from her home. For her, walking distance was forty-five minutes, even when the streets were cold. The walk along Jefferson gave her alone time to process her thoughts and decompress after work. The part-time hours did little to provide for Sierra Jackson and her son Jordan, but the commissions could be amazing. One week she brought home $1500. It didn't happen much, but occasionally, a low-key C list celebrity would stroll in for an authentic shopping experience;

an experience that guaranteed the associates wouldn't disturb them. Discretion was key in her line of work and Sierra took it to heart. She never told her friends who she sold to, but she loved wowing them with all the details. Sierra loved when design and clothes came together.

She was a stylist by nature but had dreams to create designs in her heart. Maybe one day in her future she could afford to purchase the couture she lavished other women in. The clothes were stunning. Sierra secretly tried on outfits when she closed the store. Being careful to smooth everything back out and re-hang it without flaw. She was almost home. The sun poured brightly on Sierra that late Saturday evening. It seemed to always be brightest when it was freezing outside. The snow hadn't stuck around after the last fall, but the 44-degree temperature sent chills through her Salmon colored pea coat. The sun kissed her smooth dark cocoa brown face, but it wasn't enough to keep the sting of the cold from settling on her cheeks. Sierra was a classic beauty, and she knew it. She was too modest to comment on her own good looks, but she knew how to use them to her benefit when she needed to. There was no doubt her soft looks made her White customers more comfortable. It was sad but true.

"Hey, Sea. They treating you alright at the store down there?"

Sierra's nickname was Sea, just like the ocean. One of her dreams was to see it one day. "Yes, they are Mr. Smith. I still love it. How have you been?" Mr. Smith was one of the neighborhood elders. He watched all the kids grow into adulthood. He'd lived there for 50 years and was a widower. He lost his wife of 40 years to a tiring battle with breast cancer. The entire neighborhood came together to look out for him following her death. They brought him food, did chores, whatever Mr. Smith needed. The young men still took turns mowing his lawn or shoveling his sidewalk each week. Mr. Smith ate up the attention. His wife could not have kids, so he didn't have any grandkids around. No one would know that based on all the seven-and-eight-year-old neighborhood kids that hung out on his porch. They loved listening to Mr. Smith tell stories of better times. The teenagers enjoyed the stories too, but their interest heightened when Mr. Smith spoke of the race riots that embroiled Detroit in 1943. You could see their ears perk up as they did the outdoor chores, but they were too cool to admit it.

"Just living the dream. I got no complaints." Mr. Smith sat in his rocking chair on the debilitated porch, wearing plastic thick-rimmed bifocals. He held the daily newspaper that he quickly lost interest in and sipped his black coffee. It was a habit. He knew it wasn't good for him, but a cup after dinner always satisfied him.

"I hear you, Mr. Smith. Each day is a blessing."

"Mmm. Hmm." He nodded his head. "That's shole right."

"Aren't you cold sitting out here Mr. Smith?" Sierra noticed he didn't wear coats, no matter how frigid it got. But he had a favorite cardigan. It was grey and had small initials, M.S. for Maurice Smith in the upper right corner. He shared that his wife made it for him, and it was the most comfortable piece of clothing he owned. It had frayed at the edges, but Mr.

Smith believed in sticking with what he knew. He was in fairly good health for his age and wouldn't hear of leaving his house.

"Nah, baby. The cold don't bother me. The temperature ain't that bad. My cardigan do me just fine." Sierra smiled at him. "Well, you tell your mama I said hi when you see her and to come by and join me for a cup of Joe sometime. I got that strong dark roast she likes."

It was just Folgers, Sierra laughed to herself. "I sure will tell her. You have a good night, sir." Mr. Smith nodded and brought his focus back to the newspaper. Sierra made the corner and walked up the short set of stairs that ascended to the one and half story styled house. The siding was cracking, some of the now off-white paint had peeled off, but the bones were good. It was a pleasant house. Sierra had adorned it with green, red, and silver Christmas lights. Christmas was mere weeks away and Sierra couldn't wait. It was her favorite holiday. Money was tight, but she couldn't wait to spoil her family. *Well, all the family that could be home.* She would not be sad today. She smiled at the huge red wreath with silver bells she had displayed on the outside door. Sierra's mom worked herself to the core to give her and her sister a stable home. Most times, Shandra Jackson worked three jobs at once. Cooking, cleaning, and being a second mother to kids whose parents didn't have the time or didn't want to make time for their kids. Shandra let her daughter Sierra live there because Sierra needed a safe home for her and her son. Shandra had settled into her own apartment with her wife, Debbie. Shandra saved pennies for years to buy that house. She refused to accept loan offers to buy a house near rows of abandoned homes. She finally scraped up enough money to qualify for a low-interest loan with first-time homebuyer grants. She was proud of being able to provide for her girls, but she no longer wanted all the responsibility. After Shandra paid the house off she told her daughters she wanted it to stay in the family. As long as Sierra did the upkeep, she and her two-year-old son were welcome there as long as they needed to be.

"Mommy! Mommy!" Jordan crashed smack dab into his mother's knees and barreled them in his tiny arms with a hug. He smiled from ear to ear. Sierra bent down to hug him and gave him a huge kiss on his fat cheek.

"How's my favorite Lil' man?"

Jordan laughed. "Treat, mommy?" Jordan was peering into Sierra's faux couture handbag. It was oversized with white and peach tones.

"What's this?" Sierra teased.

"Yay!"

Sierra had pulled out a plastic figurine from her bag. She loved surprising him, although he expected it now. It didn't make up for her being away, but it assuaged her guilt—just a little.

He ran off to his pile of toys in the middle of the small living room and he was full of giggles.

"Girl, you know you spoil that boy too much," Shandra said, while almost tripping over a soft block. She took her daughter into a large embrace. Sierra chuckled.

"Well, you know exactly where I get it from."

"Uh, huh? Sierra, now I told you to let me know when you were getting off so I could pick you up. Your face is freezing."

"Mom, I'm fine. I didn't want you to have to drag Jordan out in this weather. It's a short walk. You worry too much."

Shandra watched as Sierra took her coat off and hung it up; eyeing her with concern. "That's a mother's job. I'll always worry, but you gotta let people help you more. It's not easy being a single mother."

"You know I don't like being called that. Jordy has a dad. He didn't abandon us."

"Latavius, abandoned y'all the moment he got caught up in those streets, and ain't no shame in being a single mom." Shandra could see her daughter was getting frustrated. She saw the frown line forming on Sierra's forehead. "Sea, I don't want to argue with you, baby. I just want you to know that plenty of people care about you. It's okay to accept help sometimes. Nobody can raise a child on their own. Everyone leans on someone."

"I know the story, mama. You had Charmaine at 22 and I came out roaring 11 years later, making you start all over. Our dads were no good passerbys. But you love us and wouldn't trade us for the world," she teased her mother. Sierra and her sister accepted long ago that their fathers both bailed and didn't push their mother on the subject; she didn't like to talk about it and they weren't interested in dads who didn't deem them important enough to stick around.

Shandra walked toward the kitchen and pulled her strawberry cobbler out of the oven. "Now don't eat all my baby's cobbler. You know he loves it. I gotta take off, sweetie. Debbie's waiting for me, but I got your plate ready right here." She pointed to the plate covered in aluminum foil that was sitting on the front eye of the stove.

"Thank you, mama. My feet heart so bad and I'm starving. It just all smells so good."

"I still got it!" Shandra gave Sierra another hug and went to say goodbye to her grandson. At 59-years-old, Shandra did not look like anyone's grandma. She kept her hair dyed black and wore it pulled back. She carried the additional pounds that came with age, with ease. She still had her shape, and her jeans accentuated her size 14 hips and booty.

"You need anything else before I leave, baby?" Shandra yelled back.

"Bye, ma! Let me know when you get home. Tell Debbie I said hi and Mr. Smith said he wants you to come visit him," Sierra yelled back.

"I'll get over there next time." She closed the door behind her and locked it with her personal key. She walked to her parked car, with Latavius Parks on her mind. She wasn't a fan, and she wished Sierra would quit pining over him to come home, to *her* house. *He could rot in jail forever!* He knocked her baby girl up and then went to prison before Jordan made his way into the world. She couldn't stand a trifling man-and she had experience with enough of them, and a few trifling women. It took years of self-discovery and hard work before she valued herself enough to understand that she deserved better. She pulled off in her Kia truck and was looking forward to some quality time with her wife.

2

"Lane was saying you can't be accepting all those gifts from dudes you barely even know. Then I was like shit if he giving it to me, I'm taking it!" Marissa roared with laughter.

"Marissa be quiet, girl. You'll get us kicked out of court," Sierra warned.

"Girl chill, it's not like the judge is even out here. Lane ain't laying me down with diamonds, with his pretty ass," Marissa said, revealing a strong Puerto-Rican and Detroit accent. She hadn't lived around other Puerto-Rican people much in her life. Marissa was shipped from one foster home to another after she lost both her parents when she was nine-years-old and her maternal grandmother just a year later. She grew up believing anyone she got close to would be taken from her, but she made room in her heart for Lane and Sierra. She kept others at a distance; she needed to protect her heart and identity. Marissa was determined to hold on to her heritage and who she was. And she was a proud Puerto-Rican woman. She dreamed of visiting, but never had the courage to do it and face what emotions might come with such a trip.

"Why would Lane be buying you diamonds?

15

He's our friend, not our man. He got his own man, remember?"

"He deserves better than lame ass Damont, but whatever. Look, don't you love them?" Marissa showed Sierra her diamond hoops.

"They're pretty. Are they real? Might wanna do a fog test just to be sure," Sierra teased.

"Alright bish, you got jokes. Keep hating. It's all good."

"Stop it, you know I love-"

"All rise!"

Sierra and Marissa stood up. Marissa adjusted her mini-skirt up, drawing the attention of a 20-year-old defendant sitting behind her. The judge was short but large in stature. She stood five foot three but appeared much taller on the bench, leering down on everyone. The judge grabbed her gravel and banged it twice. Her skin was a dark shade of brown with a few wrinkles beginning to settle in. No hair was out of place in her short-cropped black hair with a streak of brown in the side bang. She took pride in serving at Wayne County District Court. Judge Rice had a reputation for being fair, but she was also tough and made it known when defendants appeared before her more than once. Sierra was hopeful. Latavius's attorney said they lucked out with her as the judge to hear Latavius's petition for early release. Judge Rice took her seat at the bench.

"You may be seated," said the young bailiff.

Sierra was trembling with nerves. Marissa reached over and laid her hand on Sierra's.

"It's alright, Sea. I got you."

"The court calls case 20-011-77735, State v. Parks."

"Your honor, may we approach the bench?" The question came from the prosecutor, a tall Black man dressed in a freshly pressed navy-blue suit.

"You may approach."

Latavius's attorney whispered something into his ear before walking to the bench, and Latavius nodded.

"What's going on? Why would they be going to the bench right away? I've never seen them do that. Something is wrong. I know it," Sierra said.

"Let's just wait. You know how attorneys are. They just like talking and making everything seem so secretive." Marissa felt concerned, but she couldn't let Sierra see that. Sierra was hanging all her hopes on this hearing and Latavius being home for Christmas. It was all she talked about the last two months. Latavius was eye candy, but Marissa didn't care much for him one way or the other, but as long as Sierra was happy that's all that mattered to her. The attorneys and judge were engaged and focused.

"Why is it taking so long?" Sierra whispered while staring at Judge Rice and the lawyers' backs. "I don't have a good feeling about this."

"Just hold on. Look, the lawyers are walking back to their tables now."

Judge Rice began speaking, "This case is adjourned. Call the next case please, Bailiff."

"What! What's happening?" Sierra stood. Latavius looked back at Sierra and shrugged his shoulders.

"Sierra, I'll be with you in one second. Meet me in the hall, please," the attorney said to her.

Marissa and Sierra grabbed their jackets off the wooden bench and made their way to the hallway.

Latavius's attorney, Michael Stromberg, came out a few minutes later.

"Sierra, let's go over here." He led them to a less populated corner. "It's not good news, Sierra. Can we speak alone?" Michael looked toward Marissa.

"Sea, if you need me, I'm here."

"It's okay, Marissa. I'll be fine. I'll catch up with you later. I want to visit with Latavius, anyway."

"Are you sure? I can wait."

"I'm good. I'll catch an Uber back. I'll call you afterwards."

Marissa hugged Sierra. "Okay, I'll have my ringer turned up. Good luck, girl." Marissa walked away, switching her full hips and round butt in her tiny skirt. Her sweater was just short enough to show off her tight abs and low enough to still show off her voluptuous double Ds. She loved her curves and always said J. Lo had nothing on her. She glanced back to check on her friend. She didn't focus on the lawyers, defendants, and women staring at her today. Marissa saw that Sierra was in deep conversation with Michael but holding her own. She fastened her three-quarter-length coat and was greeted by the chilly December air.

"Michael, what's going on?" Sierra asked. She liked Michael. He had twenty years of experience practicing law. He was 48-years-old and a White man who had privilege with the courts that other attorneys couldn't always access. He was not your typical public defender. He was busy, sure, but he made time for her and Latavius. She believed he genuinely cared.

"Sierra, remember we talked about how courts were releasing some inmates who had nonviolent offenses?"

"Yeah, you said it was because there were too many prisoners."

"Right. Overpopulated prisons. Latavius has a violent crime in his juvenile record. I tried to get him a waiver for that juvenile offense. I can't tell you what he did, but it should not have disqualified him. On its face it looks terrible, but the truth of the situation should have worked in Latavius's favor. He was young and made a poor decision. But Judge Rice does not like repeat offenders, and she doesn't give much weight to technicalities. I thought I could get her to make the exception. I even submitted a legal brief to her chambers before court today. She wouldn't budge. She wouldn't even hear the case."

"What? She can't do that, can she? He has a family. We need him home."

"I know. I'm not giving up. But there's only so many inmates the state will release, and Judge Rice is prioritizing first-time offenders." Sierra had her arms crossed over her chest. She shook her head and wiped a tear from her face. "Sierra, I'm not giving up. There are other options. Latavius is a good man. He deserves another chance. I won't give up on him. You can't either."

Sierra swallowed. "I won't. I'm sticking by him. I love him. It's just hard. I really need to see him. Is there anything else?"

"No, that's all. I have to get back in there. I have a full caseload today. Tell Latavius to be strong. We'll figure something out."

Sierra nodded her head in acknowledgment. She was too emotional to say anything. Sierra knew Michael was trying his best, but he had convinced her Latavius would come home. The thought of another

Christmas without him was almost unbearable. Her baby deserved to know his father from more than phone calls. She wanted to take him to visit Latavius, but he refused to let Jordan see him behind bars. Latavius told her he would reconsider when Jordan got older, but not now. *Older? How long was he going to be in there?* She didn't know what she would do if Latavius had to serve his full twenty-year sentence. Her mom had already given up on Latavius. She wanted Sierra to give Jordan a father, someone who would be there for him in real life. Sierra respected her mom, but she was wrong about that. Latavius was still a good dad. She would not take his son away from him. Sierra could feel her makeup smearing. She needed to get herself together and be strong for Latavius before she went to see him. She appreciated Michael setting up a time for her to see Latavius before he went back to Alger. Sierra looked down at her watch. She didn't have much time.

3

They were only a couple of feet apart, but the transparent barrier between them made Sierra feel like Latavius was a million miles away. The worn-down chairs were hard and uncomfortable. The room was musty and small. Sierra, filled with worry, didn't see any of that same worry in Latavius's eyes. She was perplexed but figured she was overthinking things. *Damn, it was good to see her man.* Latavius was six foot three, and his height complemented Sierra at five foot eight. His skin was a medium brown tone. He was a young Denzel Washington type of brother. Latavius was naturally charming and had a wide grin. His hazel eyes sparkled when he laughed. Oh, how Sierra loved his laugh, and his arms. They were strong and powerful, and she yearned of being wrapped up in them again. Her thoughts were drifting, and she was getting lost in his eyes.

"Sea, did you hear anything I said?" Latavius uttered, feeling annoyed.

"Hmm? Yeah, I'm listening. Keep the faith, right?"

"Yeah. You can't be worrying all the time. Ain't that what you always telling me? Have faith and all that?"

"I had faith. Faith, you would be home with

me and our baby for this Christmas. That's all. For once. Every time I get my hopes up, I just get kicked back down," Sierra said into the scuffed and heavy black phone.

"You give up too quickly. One set back is not everything. How do you think I feel? I'm the one who has to keep sitting in here, not being able to take care of my family. That shit hurts. I thought today was it too. Hell, I already packed up most of my cell."

"I'm sorry. I not trying to be selfish. I just want you home, Latavius. Jordan is getting so big. He's even trying to say da-da. He loves it when you call."

"I love talking to him too. I haven't given up though. Michael was telling me we still have options. Like they say, it's more than one way to skin a snake."

Sierra burst into laughter. "You mean more than one way to skin a cat, silly," she laughed. "Although, I kind of like snake better. I love cats."

"Girl, you crazy. But at least I made you laugh."

"You always do. But seriously, though. What options? Michael didn't tell me anything. I felt like he was being all secretive."

"Nah, it ain't like that, Sea. You know lawyers can't be violating privilege and shit. But I don't even want to get into the details. I feel like I just keep breaking your heart. But I need you to be strong and believe in me. Me and Michael, we're gonna make it happen. Judge Rice ain't the only judge out there. Another judge might be more lenient if Michael can get them to hear the case."

"But I thought she *was* the most lenient?"

"Apparently not."

Sierra asked, "What was the juvie thing Michael was talking about? He said that's why Judge Rice wouldn't give you early release."

Latavius began fidgeting with the silver phone cord. "Ahh Nah, that's just some bullshit. I was young as hell. Just fuckin' around with my boys. We got into some shit, but it wasn't like they're making it sound. That judge is biased as hell. She acts like everybody gotta be perfect. You mess up once more and she is done with yo' ass. Like she don't know what it's like to be Black."

"I got the impression it was pretty bad, otherwise you'd be coming home." She paused, giving Latavius an opportunity to explain further. He didn't. "I just can't see doing another Christmas without you. It won't even feel like a holiday. Jordan is getting older each day. He'll start remembering Christmas without you. You know that's my favorite holiday. I don't want him growing up like that. Another 18 years of this… I just don't know."

"There you go being negative again. You stuck with me all these years; this is not the time to be giving up on me. I promise you I will not be serving 18 more years just because I got caught up. I wasn't even carrying that much weight. Sentencing me way beyond the guidelines because of the muthafuckers I was with, was stupid. Carrying too much shit and running they damn mouths." Latavius shook his hand in front of the glass window. "Fuck all that, though. I'm not even trying to go there. I'm getting an early release. I didn't hurt nobody. I have served my time."

Sierra was looking down. "I want to believe that too I just-"

"Sierra, just trust me. Look at me. Please."

Sierra raised her head and her jet-black eyes met his hazel gaze. "I got this. Don't worry. I will do everything I can to get back to you and Jordan. That's on everything. Can you trust me? Please, baby. I need you."

"Christmas is only a couple weeks away. We already had Thanksgiving without you. You're asking me to believe in some Christmas miracle, like the Hallmark channel."

"Yeah, just like that."

"Oh, my goodness. You are too funny, boy. But I trust you, Latavius. You know that. Hallmark miracle it is." She was smiling.

"That's better. Even if it takes a little longer. I'll be home. Soon."

4

Detroit went from cold to freezing overnight. Sierra refused to walk home in the 30-degree temp and snow-covered streets. Detroit was hit with four inches of snow the night before, and it didn't appear to be going away anytime soon. Sierra loved winter, mostly because of Christmas, but even she wasn't courageous enough to take on that weather. Besides, it got darker quicker in the evenings during that time of year and, although she wasn't afraid of her neighbors, she was not a fool. A woman walking alone that late at night was a dangerous gamble; anyone walking alone in her neighborhood at night needed to be careful. Detroit wasn't the Motor City for everyone, and she couldn't wait until she could afford a car. The Lyft dropped her off in front of her house. She stepped into the deep snow, sloshing her off-brand Uggs and crunching through dirty snow that had already frozen over. Sierra felt pleasantly surprised to see snow-free shoveled stairs. *Theo*, she thought. *He even did the sidewalk.* Sierra felt blessed to have Theo in her life. They went way back-to the second grade. Sierra and Theo became friends after their mothers hit it off. Alicia had been a regular customer of Shandra's at a diner Shandra worked at. Theo was raised by both his mother and father, and he had a younger brother in college. Devon attended Howard University, same as Theo had. Theo and Sierra were glued at the hip ever since they met.

"Oooh, something smells amazing." Sierra didn't take a lunch break and her stomach felt like it was eating her from the inside out.

"Ah, ah, ah, don't walk in here with those dirty boots. Jordan and I took our time mopping the floor." It was aged hardwood and gleaming from the recent cleaning.

"Theo, you did not have to do that," Sierra said, kicking off her faux Uggs and taking off her winter coat and gloves. The coat had a faux fur-trimmed hood. Sierra needed to be warm, but she wouldn't do it at the cost of sacrificing fashion. She rubbed her chilly hands together. She waited outside longer than she should have had to for the Lyft. *Why did so many drivers get lost?*

"Shh. I wore Jordan out. I know you like to say goodnight, but he is out like a light. We played games, he beat me up, we cleaned, he beat me up again, ate and he clunked out."

"Theo, I don't know what I would do without you. I don't deserve you."

"I know, but I keep coming back anyway," he teased.

"I am so hungry." She walked into the kitchen and saw that Theo had a small candle lit in the middle of the kitchen table. The house was too small to have a separate dining room. He pulled her plate out of the microwave when the 60-second timer went off. "Theo, boy, you are so extra. Dinner and candles! You're always spoiling Jordan and now me. Spit it out, bruh. What's your price?"

"Sea, stop. I'm just helping my friend. I know how cranky you get when you don't eat, so I didn't really have a choice. I could either put some food in your mouth or deal with your mouth," he teased.

Sierra was already eating. "THEO! Whoo. This lasagna is on point. You know it's my favorite." She put a big scoop on a piece of buttery garlic bread and crunched into it.

"Slow down. Dang, girl. I know Miss Shandra taught you not to talk with a mouth full of food. My beautiful mama taught me how to cook. Don't let all this machismo fool you, Sea," Theo said as he playfully flexed his right bicep.

"Right, that's what it is," she laughed.

Theo was already pouring Sierra a glass of White Zinfandel. He preferred a good Cab or whiskey and gave her a hard time about her candy wine, but not tonight. He saw how tired his friend was and he knew she'd be up studying late tonight, trying to get an essay completed in time. Theo sat down and drank some of his Cabernet Sauvignon. "I ran you a bath too." Sierra opened her mouth to speak. "Stop it, enough with all the mushiness. Let me help a sista out. You only get this once a year, so don't get used to it."

"Oh, but it would be so easy to get used to! But seriously, I appreciate you watching Jordan for me while I grabbed that extra shift. I really need the money."

"How many times have I told you that I got you and Jordan? I know you're an independent woman, but you know I'm here if you need anything."

"I know Theo, we've always had each other's

backs," Sierra said. "This Zin is just what I needed, especially now that Theo's sleep." She took a nice long swallow. Theo looked at her, judging her wine preferences in silence. "Don't you say a word, boy."

"What, I'm not doing anything. Just chillin' with my friend." He had been lying to himself about that for a long time. He wasn't sure when it happened, but at some point, he felt something more, more than lifelong friends. Theo always knew Sierra was attractive, but he had never looked at her in that way. Now he could gaze at her for hours. She was stunning. He loved everything about her, and it wasn't only because she knew him better than anyone else. The way she flicked her hair from her face when she talked. That soft black hair with a hint of blue coming off it, because she always added a bit of flair to everything she did. The way she bit her bottom lip when she was nervous and how she was such a good mother to Jordan. He imagined a family with the three of them so many times, but he knew his place—that solid friend. He was only a filler until Latavius got home, but he accepted it to be closer to them. Of course, they would continue to be friends, but he imagined he wouldn't see them nearly as much if Latavius came home. These past two years were special. He would never take a man's child from him, but he loved Jordan deeply and was glad he could be there for him. But Sierra was in love with Latavius, and there was no convincing her otherwise. He had tried, subtly, but she made her position clear. She was sticking by Latavius no matter how long it would take for him to come home. He knew she was heartbroken that Latavius wouldn't be home for Christmas, but he would be there, as her friend and shoulder. Theo thought for a moment that maybe she felt the same way he did. He sensed a mutual attraction, but he was wrong. Her heart belonged to Latavius, while his heart longed for Sierra.

"I still can't believe Latavius won't be home for Christmas. Man, the system is so messed up," Sierra said.

"Yeah, but there has to be a reason they won't let him out early."

"I asked him about it, he said it was about his juvenile record, but that whatever he did as a kid-was just stupid. You know it's biased against Black men, Theo. It's not like he ever really had a chance."

"As a Black man, I do know. But I also know it's about choices and he made his." Sierra's face tensed. "Sea, I don't mean it like that. You know I want whatever you want. I hope he can come home soon and be with his family." He cringed inside as he said the words.

"I know. You're just protective. I get it." Sierra's purple and silver iPhone was buzzing. "Marissa has been blowing me up all day. She wants to go out this weekend, but I have so much to do."

"You know, that's not a bad idea. You should go out. I'll go with you."

"You-going out with the crew? Me, Lane, and Marissa?"

"Why you gotta say it like that? I work hard. I could use a break. Check out some hunnies."

"Whatever man, tell it to your crazy ex, Kisha," Sierra laughed. "She still stalking you?"

"Don't even go there. It's a date then, we clubbin' on Saturday. That's final."

"Fine, let me text her back." Her thumbs got

to work.

"Bet. But it's getting late Sea, I have some work to get done tonight. Let me clean up so you can get your bath before it gets too cold." He was already clearing her dishes, and he slightly grazed Sierra's shoulder as he did. Their eyes caught one another's for a moment too long. Sierra finally broke the stare and Theo went over to the sink.

"Man, I don't even get a foot rub tonight. Those marketing graphs can't wait? I see how it is."

"That's a special occasion only deal." *Her feet were sexy as hell*, he thought. She kept them pedicured, and they were smooth as butter.

"Thank you, Theo, for dinner and cleaning. I owe you one." She walked up to the sink and gave him a quick hug and peck on the cheek. "Don't forget to lock up," she said on her way up the stairs.

Theo yelled back, "You know I never do."

***

Sierra sunk into the warm water; the temperature was perfect. Theo had added her favorite lavender Epsom salts and her feet thanked him. She knew how lucky she was to have a friend like him. A close platonic relationship with a man and a fine ass man at that. "Mmm, mmm," she said out loud to herself. Theo was a perfect gentleman. He never made a pass at her. She wondered why he hadn't. Sierra appreciated not being harassed because that was the norm for most men she encountered. But as close as they were, she expected he might want to take things further at some point. *Maybe he didn't find her attractive*. Even if he did, it wasn't as if she could act on it in return. She committed herself to Latavius, and she was totally in love with him. *But a girl could look*. She allowed herself to sink deeper in the tub. Her hair was wrapped and protected. She spent way too long at the shop getting her deep wave Peruvian bundles installed to ruin them before Christmas, and definitely not before the nightclub. She was glad Theo was going. He went out even less than she did, and she felt secure when he was around. Marissa and Lane got wild when they partied. Theo would bring some balance and he was so easy on the eyes. She couldn't remember when he got so damn fine. She was certain that part of it was how he engaged with her son. There was nothing sexier than a man taking care of a child. Theo wasn't as muscular as Latavius, but he was the same height, lankier, but he had a broad chest and shoulders. He wore those muscle type shirts and his chest was just *there*. Her face felt warm, and she began to touch herself. She missed Latavius so badly, but she had Theo on her mind. *It's harmless*, she thought. It was her body, her mind, and a harmless fantasy. She thought of his chest, his lips, his hands, his-. "Ahh, ahhhh, ahhhh, ahhhhhhh," she softly moaned. Sierra took a few moments to catch her breath and promised herself that would be the last time.

5

The Panic nightclub in downtown Detroit made party-goers forget a tundra awaited them outdoors, and that Christmas was around the corner. It was the perfect winter escape. Situated in the heart of downtown, Panic had three sprawling floors, six dance rooms, four fully stocked bars, and a rooftop. When it was cold enough for ice to freeze over, they opened the rooftop for ice bar service. Girls, both thick and thin, danced on bar tops, teasing men while influencing them to run up their bar tabs. Strobe, laser, and beam lights came from all directions, but the deejay's lights had the most flare. The deejay was spinning her custom playlist, and she was in a good mood tonight, so she allowed some birthday shout outs. She was enjoying herself as much as the club-goers. The deejay was all about the bass. The PA speakers blasted *Lithuania*. Big Sean's and Travis Scott's lyrics filled the club, forcing everyone to scream into their friend's ear to be heard. Sierra glowed. She wore a shimmered silver dress. It was slinky and ended a few inches above her knees. She had a matching clutch. Sierra was the lucky friend responsible for holding everyone's IDs, credit cards, and phones. They almost didn't get in. Lane forgot his driver's license, and he pissed off Damont when he called him to drop it off. Damont refused to bring their sons out into the cold just so Lane could party and get drunk. Marissa *handled it* after she arrived. They knew her well at Panic and VIP access belonged to her and her crew. No IDs required.

Marissa got out of her black Uber SUV and said to them, "I told y'all to wait for me. But Nah, you'd rather stand out here and freeze."

"We don't need the editorial. Just get us in, alright," Lane said annoyingly. He dressed to the nines with skinny navy-blue slacks and a matching blazer. His shirt was ocean blue, and it looked good on him. Lane intentionally left the top two buttons undone. He was slim and tall, and his dirty blonde hair was full and swooped back at an angle. Lane finished his look with a pair of dark brown Zegna Couture's.

"Whatever, bish, come on with your no license having ass." Marissa wore all black. A tight-fitting dress that gave her the coke bottle look that she loved. Her dress didn't quite meet the top of her thighs. She refused to wear panties, including a thong. Panty lines were not an option. Her silver bracelets jingled as she walked her friends into Panic.

They had been at Panic for about an hour, and Theo still hadn't arrived. Marissa suddenly appeared from the dance floor breathing hard and made the guy standing next to her buy her a cranberry vodka, with a double shot of tequila.

"Damn girl, slow down. You know how you are when you get messy drunk."

"And how am I exactly?" Marissa tried to make a snarky comeback, but she was already feeling tipsy.

"A hot mess," Lane chuckled.

"That's okay, we'll all be a hot mess together," Sierra said. "Speaking of together, I know Theo didn't stand me up tonight." Sierra was irritated and not in the mood to dance. She was tired. She was up all night studying for her last final. Attending school online was more challenging than in person had been. On top of it, she had put in a work-shift earlier during the day. Theo promised to be there to take off some pressure of babysitting Lane and Sierra. Lane spent the entire time complaining about Damont. *Lane worried too much.* Damont married him and gave him two stepsons, Evan and Brady, but Lane was still insecure. *Was everyone around her spoiled?* Sierra thought.

"Well, look who decided to join the party?" Lane raised his vodka tonic to greet Theo.

"What's up, Lane? Hey, Marissa." Theo went to hug Sierra, and she stepped back.

"Oh, so it's like that. Come on Sea, I got caught up at work?"

"It's midnight," Sierra challenged.

"I had a deadline. Sorry, but I'm here now and I'm thirsty. I'm going to get a bourbon neat. What do you want, Sea?"

"I have to get up with Jordan in the morning. Nothing hard. Just a-"

"White Zin," Theo laughed. "I got you." *Sierra was always looking fine, but damn, he was hoping his pants didn't bulge.* Theo walked toward the bar.

Lane cleared his throat from nothing. "Excuse me, but Sea is not the only person here. We're all friends tonight. You didn't see my empty glass, Theo?" Lane said with a completely serious face.

"Lane. My bad. I'm really messing up tonight.

34

What you having my man?"

"Vodka tonic. Thank you." Lane turned his attention back to Sierra. Marissa had finished her drink and another after that. She was already back on the dance floor. Sierra watched from afar, just in case some idiot tried to take things too far. Marissa was a big girl and she could take care of herself, but she was one of Sierra's best friends and they always looked out for each other. Sierra wished Marissa would slow down. She only dated ballers and they loved having Marissa on their arm, but Sierra worried about her friend.

"Guuurrrll, that man is in love with you?" Lane said.

"What? Who?"

"Don't act coy with me. I know you're tired of hearing about Damont's ass, so let's talk about Theo. He barely noticed Marissa and I were here. His eyes were all over you."

"No, it's not like that. Theo and I are just friends. Trust me, he doesn't see me that way. He's like my brother."

"Well, you got a fine ass brother. If Damont ever leaves me, don't try to block, bish."

"For the millionth time, Damont is not leaving you. So he got a little upset because you came out tonight. It's the holidays. His wanting to be with you, boy, is a good thing."

"Yeah, I guess, but don't try to change the subject. Theo wants you, girl. You know Latavius is not coming home anytime soon. Maybe it's time for you to expand your options. I'm not close to Theo like you, but I've known him a few years now, and he seems like a good man. I know one when I see one. I got that good man radar." Lane pointed his finger at Sierra's face to emphasize his point.

"I thought you just had that horny man behavior," Sierra teased.

"Hey. I have been loyal to my husband ever since we got married. Two years now. Remember, he put a ring on it." Lane held up his left hand, showing off a stunning platinum band.

"Okay. One White Zin for you, my lady," Theo said as he handed Sierra the pink wine. "And a vodka tonic for my boy."

I'll be your boy alright, Lane thought.

"Thank you, Theo. You're so considerate," Sierra revealed a big cheesy smile.

Theo grabbed his own bourbon from the bar and took a sip. "No worries, I'm trying to have a good time tonight." Roddy Rich began blasting out the speakers. "Awww yeah, come on Sea, that's my shit." Theo pulled Sierra toward him.

She hesitated just enough and handed her wine to Lane to hold.

"Come on Lane, you joining us?" Theo asked.

Lane held up both hands and pouted his lips. "I'm on drink duty tonight. You kids have fun." *Something is going on between them and if it's not, it sure as hell will be.* Lane shook his head.

"Alright then, let's go." Theo gulped the rest of his bourbon and grabbed Sierra's hand and took her out on the dance floor. Theo dressed sensibly. He wore black slacks and a matching grey and black muscle-revealing shirt. They stayed out there for twenty minutes. That was saying a lot, given how hot and packed it was. They dragged Marissa back and a man wearing too many gold chains followed them.

He didn't get the memo that the eighties and his dreads ended decades ago.

Marissa introduced him to her friends. "This is um, um, Lar-"

"Louey," the man said.

"My friend, Louey, that's right. We're about to head out. This place is weak anyway."

"You won't be heading out with him. You're leaving with us."

"Thanks, mom, but I'm good."

"No, you're not," Sierra said to Marissa, as she grabbed her by the hand, pulling her toward her, away from Louey or whoever the hell he was.

Louey approached Sierra and went to grab at Marissa, and Theo stepped in front of the women. Lane was there a second sooner.

Louey spoke directly to Theo, ignoring Lane. "Yo, man, she's a grown woman, if she wants to go. Let her go."

"Not with you, she's not. Not today," Theo said confidently.

"It's time for you to go," Lane asserted.

"What you gone do about it with yo' fairy ass?"

"Try me," Lane said without hesitation. Lane survived an abusive father. He learned to fight at a young age and he was good at it. He spent years fighting assholes in high school and wanted a reason to knock a fool out.

Theo stepped forward and the five foot eight man stepped back. "It ain't that serious, she ain't that fine, anyway."

"Fuck you, muthafucka," Marissa slurred.

"Thanks for having my back," Lane said.

"We come together. We leave together. You okay, Marissa?"

"She's fine," Sierra said. "Let's get out of here."

They took off together a few minutes after Louey left. Lane rode with Marissa and decided she could sleep it off at his place as long as they were quiet. It would upset Damont, but he hoped to have Marissa out before Damont woke up. Damont was not a fan of Marissa. He thought she tempted Lane with her promiscuous ways. Lane thought that was ridiculous. He could not control the habits of his friends and who they slept with was their business-well his business too because he liked to know everything, but Damont was off base. Lane appeared confident and wild, but he was more insecure than most knew.

Theo shared a Lyft with Sierra. They both sat in the backseat. The driver wasn't talkative, and they didn't mind. "I'm sorry I was so late."

"Oh, it's fine. Don't worry about it. Just don't let it happen again. I was beginning to think you stood me up?" she laughed.

"I would never do that to you. I love being-I mean, I always have a good time with you. I'm glad you invited me. I needed that more than I thought. Needed to relieve some stress. My mom keeps telling me I work too hard."

"You do, but I'm no better. And what happened to Kisha? I thought you were still doing the late-night 'U up' booty calls with her."

"You funny, Sea. That Zin got your trippin'. Alright."

"Quit being so serious. I'm messing with

you." Sierra put her hand on Theo's and looked him in the eyes. "I appreciate you, bro."

Theo felt a stab in his gut when Sierra said "bro" but he also noticed she kept her hand on his for the entire ride. He wanted to take her right there in the back seat. *Her dress was so tiny and those legs*. Theo felt himself growing, and this time he didn't care if Sierra noticed.

6

Latavius led his mom to the small grey open back seats in the visiting room. The guard kept careful watch until they sat down. For good reason, they suspected Eve was sneaking contraband into the prison through Latavius. She had in the past, but she didn't today. Her son was a good kid, but he needed to make a living to survive at Statesville-besides things were looking up-she expected that her son would come home soon. Eve sat across from Latavius and worked hard to ensure she didn't touch him. They ignored the checkers and books for children that set to the left of them and the people to the right and behind him. It was easy with the big wide and white support post divider. Weekend visiting was always busy, but they were fortunate that the seats directly next to them were unoccupied. They had important matters to discuss.

"Mama, you know I didn't have that much weight," Latavius whispered. "20 years for a few grams of cocaine. That's bullshit. You know they tacked everything on to me for that punk Junior. Criminal financial enterprise-just because I was with him. How am I responsible for his shit? Five for carrying heat on me because of that juvenile bullshit. But I'd rather do time than be out there caught slippin'. For real, though."

"Latavius, you are not doing 20 years for no damn body. Fuck them. They'll have their day."

"Shit, they locked up too, so we all having our day, but I'm getting this early release. Watch me."

"Latavius," Eve began whispering. "I told you last time you need to consider that offer. They don't happen every day."

"Mama, I love you, and I know you want me home, but I ain't no snitch. I'll die before I go out like a bitch. That's on everything."

Eve looked around to see if anyone was paying attention. The other families were heavily engrossed in their own visits, and a newborn was crying. The noise concealed their conversation. "Boy, you sound crazy as hell. How do you think you're going *out* in here after 20 years? You're always talking about Sierra and how you want to get back to her and Jordan, not that she ever takes any time to drive down to see you. But back to my point, you need to think. Those prosecutors are not letting go of your juvenile record. You're lucky you even got approached. You have a good public defender this time. That pitiful boy you had at trial wasn't worth a damn."

"Mama, I told you to get off of Sierra's back. You know she don't have a car and I told her not to bring Jordan."

"So she can't bring herself either?"

"Mama! Stop."

"Damn. Alright. Calm down. Shit. I don't have time for Sierra, anyway. I need to get back before it gets too dark with all the snow out there."

"I still have another appeal-ineffective assistance of counsel. I have options. Besides, Michael told me I still can get an early release. Might not be by the holidays, but I sure as fuck won't be here until my son is grown. It's cats in here going crazy, and they haven't even served a dime. That's not my future. But a snitch. Hell, Nah! I'm not doing no troll ass 6ix9ine sideways shit. I would be dead before I hit the streets. Shit, I would kill my damn self."

"Don't you ever say that," Eve chided. She sighed in frustration. *How did I raise such a dumb child?* Eve had kept a stash of heroin and oxycodone in her freezer for years and she managed the pull tabs at a local bar. Her legit work didn't pay the bills, but she appreciated the cover it provided. She didn't consider herself a drug dealer, just a woman providing for hers. The few men she dated sure weren't bringing in any real money. Eve was 65-years-old and preferred her freedom over commitment, and Eve loved her son. He was her heart. Her square daughters moved away, but Latavius was a mama's boy. He stayed close to home. "I know you don't really believe the courts care if your Black ass had a fair trial. Guilty in two hours. Uh-uh. You're risking too much. I can't force you to do anything. You're a grown man now." Eve subconsciously rubbed her forearms. The visiting room was always cold. "But Michael talked to me." Latavius look at his mom suspiciously. "He didn't tell me anything subject to privilege. His words. But he assured me that no one would find out. They would make it look like a legitimate early release, but it would be a *different* type of early release, you know what I mean, son?"

Latavius was done with the conversation. He knew how hard-headed his mama was when she got an idea in her head. She had good intentions, but she was wrong about this. She wasn't even thinking about the heat it would bring her. She was asking him to do the unthinkable. "Yo, mama, what you think about my new kicks?"

Eve peered at her son in his pressed blue-collar shirt and pants. "I like them, Latavius. You must have just got those. They're as white as the snow, not a scuff on them," Eve laughed. "You were always crazy about your tennis shoes."

Latavius looked up and nodded at the guard walking through the aisle, who monitored everyone in the visiting room. He couldn't stand him, but he needed some peace until he could get out of that hellhole. "Yeah, I got 'em last week. Thanks for coming through for me. You look good, mama. I can't wait to come home and get a real meal. I want a fat juicy burger."

"I can do better than that. Nothing but the best for my son. Steak, lobster, potatoes; it'll be a buffet." Eve needed some assistance from her son and looked forward to him getting out. Soon, she hoped. She didn't need a lot of help, just recruitment for new customers. Eve didn't believe in snitching, but she couldn't fathom her son being locked up for the next two decades. She needed him. Christmas Eve was the next day and she couldn't go through it without first visiting her son.

The guard heard just enough to infer that Latavius was planning on snitching out his co-defendants. He struck pay dirt. That kind of information was worth a lot, and the state wasn't paying him enough to keep his mouth shut.

The guard tapped Latavius on the shoulder. "Alright, mama let's go take these pictures."

7

"Oww-eee!" Kayla cried.

"Mommy, Davon hit Kayla in the head," Marcus said in a high-pitched whine and pointed while pointing at Davon.

"Not on purpose. Marcus quit lying! It was the ball." Davon said in defense. The five-year-old was adorable, especially when he was upset. Three-year-old Kayla sat pouting puppy dog style with her bottom lip poked out and her hand on top of her forehead.

"Alright, that's enough. Davon, how many times have I told you not to play ball in the house? Apologize to your sister," Charmaine said. She walked over to Kayla and kissed her forehead.

"Sorry, Kayla," Davon said with his head held down.

"Boys, you have one more chance or playtime is over. I'm serious. It's almost bath time, anyway. And put that ball back up," Charmaine ordered.

"See Davon. You always get us in trouble," Marcus continued whining.

"Marcus, enough with the lip. You're the oldest. Stop all that whining. Now go play. Grown-ups are talking," Charmaine said.

Jordan looked confused and scared. He didn't have siblings at home and didn't go to traditional daycare, so he wasn't used to seeing much arguing. Sierra was rubbing Jordan's head as he stood close to her side. "It's okay, Jordan, you can go play. Auntie bought you new Legos," Charmaine said with a wide smile. Jordan smiled and looked at his mother for approval.

"It's okay, Jordy, go play with your cousins." Sierra held both of his baby cheeks in her hands and kissed him on top of his head. Jordan scuttled off back to the playroom to be with his cousins.

Sierra sat at the six-person walnut dining room table next to her sister, Charmaine Hughes. She was drinking a can of Sprite and finishing her banana pudding. "Charmaine, I don't know how you do it. I barely manage and I only have one," she said, taking another bite of banana pudding.

"Girl, they bad as hell," Charmaine laughed. "But those are my babies. My world."

"I know they are, and Jordy is mine, but it's so much work. Sometimes I don't know if I'm doing the right thing or not."

"Babysis, you'll never know. You just have to do the best you can. Listen to mama. I know she can get on our nerves, but she knows what she's talking about."

"I don't know what I would do without mom," Sierra replied. "I can't even imagine."

"Well, you can thank mama for that banana pudding you've been dogging out. I still use her recipe."

"I thought I had enough at Thanksgiving, but you know I can't resist it! Sierra grinned. "And I appreciate that you hosted Thanksgiving for the second year in a row. I know it's a lot-but it helped since Latavius couldn't be home." Charmaine took a sip of her black coffee and met her sister's eyes.

"Sea, we are all here for you-until, when, and if, Latavius comes home. Me, mama, Eddie. You know he loves his nephew like one of our boys. And you have Theo, too. You'll never be alone. You're family."

Sierra was twirling her spoon needlessly over the remnants of vanilla wafers and banana pudding left on her plate. "I appreciate everybody, for real. I have good friends. I don't know what I'd do without Theo and Marissa and Lane. They're like family too. But you are so lucky to have Eddie. A dedicated husband at home and he's crazy about you. I want that."

"Girl, Eddie's not perfect. He's out there right now trying to find the Black baby doll he forgot to get Kayla for Christmas," she chuckled. "But I am blessed. He's a good man. And a lucky man. I'm a bomb wife and mom. Three kids and I still fit into my size sevens, ass and all." Charmaine was trying to lift her sister's spirits, but she saw Sierra's sullen face hadn't changed. Charmaine said, "Sea, look at me." Sierra turned her head to look at her sister.

"Latavius will come home one day. I know it didn't happen for the holidays as you wanted, but you're my baby sister and I don't want you spending the rest of your life pining over a man who's behind bars. You have a son and you're so young. You have your entire life ahead of you. I'm always telling my 11th graders they have to live each day to the fullest. Have dreams and goals-but always do for yourself.

Look at what's around them that they may be missing.
That's why I still don't understand why you are so
worried about Latavius when Theo is right there. He's
a good man, Sea, and I think he's in love with you."

Sierra stood up to wash her plate.
"Charmaine, I'm not one of your students. You
always feel like you need to teach me a lesson. I'm not
here for that. I just wanted some time for me and
Jordy to have with our family before Christmas Eve.
And you know what else, you and Mama need to stop
trying to push Theo on me. I love Latavius. I'm *in*
love with Latavius. He is Jordy's father, and he is who
I will have a life with. He will come home." Sierra
started balling at the kitchen sink with the yellow
sponge crushed beneath her small hand.

Charmaine sat her mug of coffee down and
walked over to her sister. She embraced Sierra in a
hug. "It's okay, baby sis. I know it hurts. I love you.
I'm here. No more talk about Theo. I promise."

Charmaine stood only a couple inches taller
than her sister, but the emotional strength she
provided to her family was akin to a giant. Charmaine
was a nurturer. Mom, teacher, and wife. She loved it
all. Charmaine felt so grateful that she could have a
family and a career. She had high standards, she was
no one's pushover. Charmaine would give a person in
need- her last dime, but she would not be played for a
fool or be taken advantage of by anyone. Her
husband, Eddie knew this. He didn't dare try to run
games on Charmaine that he did with other women
before they settled down.

Eddie was a hard-working mechanic, and
together they provided a home to their children in a
local Detroit suburb. The four-bedroom home had a

large backyard for their kids and the dog the kids wanted for Christmas. It met their needs. The house was close enough for both their families to visit, most importantly their mothers and Eddie's father. Family was important to them both. But their marriage and kids were their first priority. Charmaine was confident that Eddie would not risk his life with her for any one-night stand or something extra on the side like other men did. She was confident in their love, and she knew how to satisfy her man's needs like no one else.

Eddie was her soul mate, and she believed Theo was Sierra's, but her sister wouldn't hear of it. Sierra was wasting her life waiting around for Latavius. He'd made his choices, but they shouldn't be Sierra's sacrifices. *It wasn't right.* Regardless of Charmaine's feelings, she knew she would be there for her sister. "Come on, Sea. Don't worry about those dishes. I'll make Eddie do them later."

Sierra laughed and walked back to her chair at the table. "You always making Eddie clean up. That poor man."

"Poor my ass. He got it made. He better appreciate all the good loving he gets at home."

"You're so damn conceited. Thanks for being here, Charmaine. It's not that I'm ungrateful, I'm just all over the place. Latavius promised me he would be home this time. I know it's not his fault, but I'm still mad at him. And Theo, he's texting me now, checking in on me and Jordy. I feel guilty sometimes, for real. It's not fair to him to be filling in for another man, but at the same time, I appreciate him so much. Jordan needs that male figure in his life. Maybe I'm just selfish."

Charmaine handed Sierra another Sprite and some Kleenex. "You're not selfish. And unfortunately, Latavius can't control anything. I hate to say this, but it's all wishful thinking on his part. That boy did something bad in his past. The state is not letting him out." Sierra looked at Charmaine in disbelief. "Not forever, I just mean not right now. One day, maybe sooner than I think. Who knows? But as far as Theo goes, that boy cares about you-" Charmaine felt Sierra's glare.

"You brought him back up, Sea. I'm just saying I haven't lived 35 years and not learned what a man in love looks and acts like. My point is, don't worry about him being there for you. He enjoys it. You make him happy and I *think* he makes you happy." Charmaine threw her hands up. "But I'm going to stop, no lectures from big sis."

"Thank you."

"Don't get smart now. You can still, what the kids say these days…catch these hands?" They both burst into laughter.

"Mama!!! Kayla bit me!" Marcus screamed.

"Ooh child, that boy is still whining at 7-years-old." Jordan ran back into the dining room, sensing trouble.

"Leave him alone, Charmaine. He's just sensitive," Sierra said as she picked up Jordan.

"Yeah, that's my baby. I'm coming, Marcus," Charmaine answered. "I'm so glad you're spending the night. Now, help me bathe these Bebe's kids and get them to bed so we can gossip and drink some wine. I got your White Zinfandel in the fridge."

"This is why I love you," Sierra giggled.

8

DETROIT, 2017

***

Sierra had just found out she was pregnant. Shock was not a strong enough word to describe her current state.

"Ooh yes, I am NOT pregnant. Yes, yes, yes. This body is staying tight!!!" Marissa jumped up and down and she hugged Sierra like an excited five-year-old. Marissa was doing her happy dance in front of the medical clinic. "The doctor gave me a new favorite word, negative. I felt like I was on Maury Povich and he just told me I am NOT the father." Marissa was so giddy she didn't notice Sierra's glum expression.

"Marissa, being pregnant is not the end of the world. People have babies every day. It's not even that serious," Sierra said.

Marissa's smile disappeared. "Damn Sea, you can't be happy for a bish for once. Why you be hatin' so much? You are my best friend. Be happy for me. Shit."

"Marissa, I'm not hatin' on you. I came here with you because I'm your best friend. You were scared as hell, remember?"

"And,what's your point. I'm not pregnant so-
"

"So, you made me take a test to support you, for fun."

"Oh my gosh, Sea. You're so damn dramatic. *Dramatica!*"

"I'm not being fucking dramatic!"

"Then what's your damn prob-" Marissa covered her mouth with her hand. "Estás embarazada! La Trampa!" Marissa was giggling.

"You called me a what?"

"Sea, are you pregnant?" Marissa asked seriously.

"I can't believe this shit. I was so careful. I'm still having my period. I mean it's been lighter, but it's been there. I literally took the test for fun to support you. This cannot be happening. I cannot deal with this shit right now."

"I thought you were on the pill."

"I am on the pill and I use protection...mostly."

"Damn, girl. You cannot be sliding on that, for real."

"Seriously? We were here because of you."

Marissa ignored Sierra's comment. "Is it Latavius's baby?"

"Yes, bitch! Latavius. Who else would it be? Oh, my gosh."

"I ain't saying nothing. I'm just saying."

"Well, you can stop just saying, anything," Sierra replied impatiently.

"Sierra, it will be fine. Quit freaking out. Latavius loves you. He's not going anywhere. Come on. Let's not do this in front of the clinic."

They began walking away from the downtown clinic. It was 80 degrees out and they were not in a rush. They both wore sundresses, that day and the sun was shining brightly upon them. At 21-years-old, they had their whole lives to look forward to. Marissa felt relieved for herself, but newly worried for her friend.

Sierra felt the weight of the world on her chest. "My mom is going to kill me. This was one of her biggest fears. That one of her daughters would get knocked up with no ring and no degree. I've barely started college and you know how she feels about Latavius. How can I have a baby?"

Marissa stopped at the 'Don't Walk' sign and turned toward Sierra, "Sea, you just found out five minutes ago. Ms. Shandra is going to be fine. It's not like she'll disown you. You're a grown-ass woman. But you need to talk to Latavius first. Make sure *he* is down with you and steps up if you decide to keep it."

"Latavius would never abandon me, especially with his baby." Sierra paused in mid-thought. "What do you think? Should I keep it?"

The light changed, and they walked across the street. They paused their conversation until they were out of earshot of the other pedestrians.

"I can't tell you what to do. You know I did not want a baby, but I could never kill it. I lost my family way too young, so it's just not something that I could do. But you gotta do what's best for you. Either way, I'm here and I got auntie duties covered if you have that gigantic head baby." Sierra gave her a friendly nudge in the side. "What? You know you gotta big head girl."

"Shut up, let's grab a burger. Now I know why I've been eating so much lately." Marissa cut her eyes in Sierra's direction. "Don't even think about saying something! And by the way, it's auntie's treat."

***

Sierra waited two days to tell Latavius. She knew he should be the first to know, but she confided in Charmaine first. Her sister would know what to do. She was about to deliver her third child. Charmaine was supportive. She didn't judge her.

"Sea, having a baby at any age is scary and yes, I wish you were older, just so you could live more of your life the way you want to, but you and the baby will have all of us, including mama. Trust me, mama wouldn't want you to have an abortion. That would break her heart more." Charmaine paused. "At the beginning and end of the day, it's your decision but you need to tell Latavius. I'm not his biggest cheerleader, but I hope he'll step up."

Sierra went to see Latavius the next day. She met up with him at his cousin Roe's house. They had the house to themselves. Latavius was all over her before and after she broke the news to him.

"Sea, you having my baby. Why would I be upset? I love you, Sea. I'm not trying to get caught up with these other hoes. They'll throw a baby on you quick."

"Other? Excuse me," Sierra protested.

"Nah, baby, not like that. You're my princess. All that's in the past, you're my future. You and our baby." Latavius bent his head down to kiss Sierra's stomach.

"Latavius, I'm not even sure if I'm keeping it.

I don't think I'm ready for a baby. Are you?"

"It's too late to be ready. The baby is ready for us. We have our moms, our fam, shorty will be alright."

"You can't be in the streets either. You know I don't like that. If we have a baby-you know how these streets are. I worry about you enough as it is." Sierra was almost in tears.

"I promised you I'm almost done with this. I barely even sell anything anymore. Nothing serious. I'm going to get my two-year degree like I told you. I'm going to be an electrician. I'm not meant for these streets. Everybody fake as hell. I want more than that. Especially now."

"You've been promising since I was nineteen. This is serious now. You need to be serious. We're not kids anymore."

"I'm serious as a heart attack. I'll start looking for jobs today if that's what you want. Just let me move this little bit of weight so I don't owe these clowns nothin'." Sierra's face softened, but she still appeared concerned. "Sea, I can't be owing anybody anything. Muthafuckas get killed for that every single day. I need to see this through. After that. I'm going legit. Real talk. Those streets don't mean a damn thing to me. My world is right here beside me."

"Okay, but this is it. No more games."

Latavius took a puff of his joint.

"And you have to quit smoking that around me now."

"So you *are* keeping my baby?" he said as he put the joint out in the ashtray.

"I didn't say all that, but just in case, you know."

They were sitting on the couch. It was well-worn and had a faded toasty brown color.

Latavius reached over to kiss Sierra. "What I know is I've been craving you all damn day. I think you're even finer pregnant."

"Yeah, I don't think it works like that-but I do want you, so what are you are waiting for?"

Latavius literally jumped at the invitation. My B.E.D, by Jacquees played from the iTunes playlist through the living room speakers. Latavius had made love to enough Black women to know better than to run his fingers through Sierra's hair, and he was a generous lover. He threw her legs up, leaned forward between them, and delicately thrust his tongue where Sierra liked it most. He tasted her wetness, as her moans vibrated in his mouth.

Sierra grabbed him by his full head of hair, "I don't want you to make love to me, Latavius. I want you to fuck me, hard." She peered directly into his eyes and he did not question her command.

Latavius raised up and kissed her ferociously. She followed his tongue and covered it with hers. Their mouths were wet and hot and thirsty for more. Latavius propelled himself inside of her. Hard, as she demanded. Fast, like she wanted. He filled her, and she tightened around him, juices flowing freely. Latavius was young but disciplined. He listened for her purrs of satisfaction before exploding inside of her.

"I love you, baby," he whispered in Sierra's ear.

"I know. I want you to just stay here-inside of me, a little longer."

"Where else would I be?"

9

Sierra ached for Latavius. His touch. His laugh, especially the way he made her laugh. But one thing she didn't miss was his meddling mother. Eve sent Sierra a shady text about how she visited Latavius the day before and aimed an innuendo at Sierra that she and Jordan should have also been there. Eve conveniently forgot that Latavius refused to see Jordan behind bars.

Eve was all talk. She rarely saw Jordan. Sierra didn't keep him away, but Eve was only reachable when she wanted to be. It was usually when she had negativity to spread. Sierra learned to avoid Eve's nasty glares and condescending comments, but she refused to be one of Eve's pawns.

Sierra asked her mom to be the intermediary and to take charge of coordinating Jordan's visiting arrangements with Eve. Shandra didn't hesitate. She was very protective of Sierra and refused to let someone like Eve hamper her daughter's emotional stability or rob her of one moment of joy. It worked out nicely. Shandra was Eve's match, and Eve knew she couldn't rattle Shandra. Eve picked her grandson up and dropped him off at Shandra's. It was all business, no fuss. That was best. It protected Jordan from the infighting without making anyone out to be the bad guy. Besides, it was a rare occasion when Eve actually wanted to see Jordan.

Sadly, Sierra realized that there weren't any family members, hers or Latavius's, that truly supported their relationship. At best, they all put up with it. Latavius was not a bad person and they both lived in their share of shady neighborhoods. Latavius grew up in the Sojourner's Truth Housing Project on the eastside of Detroit. He had to do what he needed to in order to survive. He never planned for it to be lifelong, but he was introduced to the game at a very young age. Sierra knew he didn't enjoy it, but everyone was so judgmental. Except, her close friends. They weren't jumping up and down for her and Latavius, but they knew she was happy and respected it.

Sierra pushed her negative thoughts out of her head. It was the holiday season, and it always flew by faster than she wanted. It was Christmas Eve. She needed to enjoy it. She was fortunate that two of her closest friends in the world came to help her give Jordan an amazing Christmas morning. They spoiled Jordan in the best way, and she needed all hands on deck to help her wrap gifts for Santa's delivery.

"Earth to Sea." Lane snapped his fingers. "Girl, did you hear anything I said?"

"Yes, I heard you," Sierra answered, fully aware she barely heard anything Lane said. "You want that new Call of Duty Black Ops and hope Damont bought it since we didn't."

"Uh-no. That's not what I said. I said I hope Damont got the PS5 and you heifers slipped by not getting me the game."

Marissa chimed in, "It's the thought that

counts, boy. It's not as if Call of Duty, screams out as the gift to give you. Just say it next time. All these hints aren't working. We thought you wanted that black blazer, and it wasn't cheap. So ungrateful, I swear."

"Oh, no you just didn't bish," Lane replied. "What? I'm not supposed to bond with my sons? I can't appreciate video games because I'm a gay man? Somebody wearing her stereotypes loud tonight."

Marissa threw Christmas wrapping at Lane's head, and Sierra followed her lead. Boxes and toys surrounded them with dozens of rolls of Christmas wrapping paper, bows, tape, scissors, bags, and other Christmas decor. R&B Christmas tunes played while they joyfully fought, wrapped gifts and reminisced. The artificial tree was a snow-covered white ensemble. It stood seven-feet tall, adorned in tones of blue and silver, with soft pink accents. Sierra insisted on keeping it stylish. She even insisted that everyone have their own signature wrapping paper, which she chose and bought.

"Lane, you're more obsessed with these video games than the kids!" Sierra teased.

"Yeah, choose a lane, Lane!"

"Oh, you're really getting it now, and don't you think about taking my blazer back," Lane laughed as he playfully launched more decor at Marissa and then Sierra. They were in a full-on Christmas fight and the ladies were playfully wrestling Lane when the door lock turned.

"Oh, well, don't let me interrupt-I can come back later," Theo said as he pointed his thumb back toward the door. Sierra threw a wad of Christmas decor at him. "It's like that? Okay."

"Come on in, Theo, we're just finishing up the gifts for Jordy. So he knows Santa came on time," Sierra said.

"Oh, that's what this is? Because it kind of looked like-"

"Let me stop you right there," Lane said. "I mean they're gorgeous and all but not my type."

"Fuck you, Lane, I'm everybody's type," Marissa exclaimed. She looked up at the gigantic box Theo placed at his feet. "Theo, what is that? Did you put Santa in the box?" she laughed.

"It's that the new Power Wheels Ford F-150 for my Lil' man. In other words..." Theo cleared his throat with a fake cough, "me putting y'all to shame," Theo said while revealing a wide grin.

"Theo! That is way over the top. I know Jordy is spoiled and I'm okay with that, but I want him to realize time and family matter way more than the gifts, as he grows up. He's only two. I don't even know what to say."

"That's easy. That Uncle Theo only got him one gift-just one Sea-but also the best gift."

"Damn. Theo making baby daddy moves," Marissa said.

Lane reached over to meet her high-five. "It's one toy, Sea. Jordan will be fine. He won't even remember all this, anyway." Everyone looked at Lane. "What? I have kids too. This is for us more than them. I'm just being honest, but I love it and besides I had my kids' gifts ready weeks ago. No shade. Seriously." Lane stood up to make himself another glass of vodka soda.

"Sit it in that corner, Theo," Sierra commanded. Theo stepped forward. "No, no, no, take off those wet boots first." Theo slipped off his boots by stepping down on one boot with the back of his heel of the other. "I don't know how I'm supposed to fit it with that by the tree. It's just so big. Thank goodness you wrapped that thing."

"Of course, I got you, Sea," Theo said a bit too loudly, like a gleeful kid on Christmas.

"Thanks, but we have to quiet down y'all. I don't want Jordy to wake up and learn who Santa truly is." She bit down into one of the Buttery Spritz Christmas cookies that Charmaine made for them and ate a reindeer's head.

Marissa was texting and sipping on Sauvignon Blanc. She and Lane refused to touch their girl's White Zinfandel and Sierra didn't mind. It was more for her. Marissa stood up to help Theo situate the enormous gift. "Theo, let me help you. You're doing it all wrong," Marissa said. "¡Tal ameteur!"

"¿Quieres ver sobre eso?" Theo replied.

Marissa's expression instantly transformed to shock and intrigue.

"Yes, mama. I know a little Español," Theo charmingly said, with apparent pride.

Taken aback, Sierra was staring at Theo and Marissa.

"Sea come join me in the kitchen for a second," Lane ordered. Sierra walked over to Lane without hesitation.

"Girl pick your face up. Yes, he is flirting with Marissa and why should it matter to you? You've made it clear you don't want him, remember?"

"Lane, stop. I was just surprised that's all. I didn't think Marissa was his type. I don't know what he said, but the way he said it. Whatever. I'm with

Latavius, anyway. Why would I care? I just don't want Theo to get hurt."

"Damn Sea, you got them walking down the aisle already. They are two grown-ass people. Let that go. Unless you *do* want him. And if that's the case, then you need to tell Marissa. Not that I think she'd go for Theo, anyway. He does well, but he's not bringing home enough coins for a girl like Marissa." Sierra was still staring at Theo and Marissa while they struggled to figure out what to do with the large box and other gifts. "Sierra, I need to talk to you. I didn't call you in here to talk about those two. I have a serious problem. I need your advice. Can we talk privately?"

Sierra turned her head back towards Lane. "Yes, of course, let's talk in my room." Sierra was about to yell to Theo and Marissa that they were going upstairs, but they were laughing and engaged with each other. They weren't paying attention to Sierra and Lane.

They made it to Sierra's room and sat on the foot of the bed. Lane's face-absent of its usual cheery demeanor-was flat and despondent. Sierra picked up on the change right away.

"Lane, did something happen? You look so serious. What is it? Are you okay?"

Tired of pretending that he had his life figured out, Lane laid it all out on the table. "I think Damont is planning to leave me," he mumbled.

"What?! No. Lane. How? Why? What did you do?"

"Thanks a lot, Sea. Just the supportive friend I need."

"Lane, I'm sorry. I don't mean it like that. I

know you fuss and complain over Damont a lot, but I thought you two were happy. And you have the boys. I'm surprised. That's all. You really think he's leaving?"

"We've been off for a long time. I feel like I'm getting the cold shoulder. I'm always walking on eggshells around him. And he still complains whenever I go out with y'all or Marissa. We don't even go clubbing as much as we used to. I'm a dad now. I have responsibilities. I don't think of Brady and Evan as my step kids. It's my first marriage, Sea. I don't want a second." Lane stopped talking to wipe his eyes with the back of his hand. Sierra gently stroked and focused her complete attention on her friend. "I see him spending more time with his ex-husband. I know Thomas has the right to see his kids, but he is always lurking around somewhere. Damont always accuses me of cheating and you know I've been faithful, Sea. I left all that other bullshit in my past when we got married. When we hooked up, he was the married one, not me."

"That's true. You're a good husband and father. This is not on you."

"Now, every night is a late work night. I don't know of any court hearings or client meetings that happen at midnight. It's a regular occurrence now. Something is going on. Either he's planning to get back with Thomas or he's messing around with someone else. That's probably why he's accusing me." Lane was talking through his tears. "We haven't made love in two months. Am I tripping, Sea?"

Sierra met Lane's gaze. Lane didn't deserve this. He was a good man with a loving heart. Even at his saddest point, he was still strikingly handsome.

Damont was a fool, and he wasn't worthy of Lane. Damont was cheating with Lane when he was married to Thomas, and Thomas left him because of it. Lane still carried guilt about it. Sierra always thought Damont was too old and experienced for Lane. He was approaching 50-years-old and had a ready-made family. Sierra adored Evan and Brady, so did Marissa, and they were wonderful with Jordan. They treated him like a baby brother. But Damont wasn't having any of it. He dismissed Lane's friends as if they were annoying misfits. He never took time to get to know the people who cared about Lane the most. He spoke to Lane's parents just enough to keep the peace. Sierra spoke to Lane's mom, Kathryn, about Damont. She made it clear that she and Lane's stepfather both supported him, even though Damont was almost their age. In reality, Kathryn thought Damont was an asshole but swore Sierra to secrecy. Kathryn never wanted her son to doubt her love, especially given the abuse he survived from his father. She carried her own guilt.

"No, you're not tripping. I hope it's not what you think. I want you to be happy but know your life is not over if Damont turns out to be an ass wipe." She tried to make him laugh, to no avail.

"You sound like Marissa did when I told her."

"Good. Marissa knows what she's talking about."

"But I come from a family of divorce. I don't want that, and I can't do this to my boys. Two divorces. No way. They didn't do anything wrong. Hell, I didn't anything wrong."

"You know what, it's Christmas Eve, and it is not going down like this. You are ridding yourself of

63

all that damn negativity, all your speculation, and you are going to get wasted my friend. Tall vodka soda coming up."

"Sea, you don't know how to make a damn vodka soda," he laughed. "But I'm going to drink that bish, anyway."

They returned downstairs and saw Marissa and Theo putting on their coats. "All done!" Marissa said. "And clean too." Sierra was silent. "You're welcome, woman!"

"Are you guys leaving?" Sierra asked, disappointed and confused.

"Theo was taking off, so I'm bumming a ride with him. Lane, you have to Uber back without me. Sorry, not sorry."

"I see you, Marissa. Abandoning me for the next man."

"Oh, shut up and come and hug me, boy," Marissa said to Lane.

"I should get out of here too. It's late and I need to be up early with the boys tomorrow," Lane echoed. He quickly ordered up his Uber.

Everyone began embracing each other in goodbye hugs while wishing each other a Merry Christmas. Sierra thanked everyone for showing up and helping. Sierra gave Theo his goodbye hug as Marissa opened the front door to leave. Marissa's face instantly froze over from the sight before her. The man did not acknowledge Marissa and strolled past her into the house.

"I'm home, Bae. Somebody ordered a Hallmark miracle?"

Sierra didn't believe her ears, but she knew that voice better that her own. She abruptly pushed

Theo away and turned toward the voice.
"Latavius?"

AFTER THE MIRACLE

10

Six weeks ached by with painful precision. But it wasn't all bad. Sierra was on clouds the first two weeks after Latavius came home. She floated in the air, walked in the air, and became one with it. She had her dream Christmas, better than she could have imagined, and a fun New Year's Eve. Well, New Year's Eve night wasn't that great, but making up was. Sort of.

Dumbfounded wasn't close to describing Sierra's state of surprise when Latavius showed up at her door on Christmas Eve. She had given up on her boyfriend coming home, but there he was standing right in front of her. It was a joyous night. They stayed awake until the sun rose. Talking, peeking in on Jordan, sleeping, and making love. Three times-she counted. Sierra enthusiastically welcomed Latavius to her bed, snuggled up in his powerful arms with his muscles securing her as if she was his gift. Christmas was almost perfect, but Sierra had to explain why she was in Theo's arms. She told Latavius that she was saying goodbye to everyone, including Theo, when he walked in. It was nothing more than two friends parting ways. Latavius had always been jealous of Theo, and until recently Sierra felt flattered Latavius was so protective. However, she did not enjoy spending a good portion of her Christmas Eve reunion explaining to her man that one of her best friends was simply that.

Sierra knew Theo much longer than she had known Lane and Marissa; she met them in high school. Latavius didn't let Jordan touch Theo's Christmas gift. He stored the truck away on Christmas morning. The jealousy didn't feel cute anymore. It was almost as if Latavius wanted to cut the one person out of her life who had been a fill-in for him in so many ways, and she genuinely cared for Theo. Sierra couldn't imagine life without him, and she would not be forced to choose between two of the most important men in her life.

Latavius was her lover, and she cherished that, but it wasn't the same as it once was. He moved the same, smelled the same, but he wasn't sensual, not like he used to be. Latavius used to know every part of her body. He knew what made her purr and more importantly, he knew what made her scream. That Christmas Eve, she blamed her shortcomings on all the talk about Theo. The tension from the subject surely made her less focused and attentive, except it hadn't gotten better.

Latavius had been home for six weeks and she faked more orgasms than she could count, except for that one time. Hot blood rushed through her body with the shame she felt each time she thought about it. Theo-he had entered her mind as Latavius expanded her from the inside out, and the lust she experienced was irresistible. Ashamed and satisfied, she gave her man the only orgasm she had since he came home. She wasn't sure if he knew she faked climaxes, but believed he suspected. When they made love, he didn't engage with her and no longer looked her in the eyes. He turned off the lights when he knew she preferred them on-all the time. Two weeks had passed since they last had sex. Latavius approached her sometimes, but he accepted her rebuffs easily. He didn't put up a fight. Maybe he was still upset over New Year's Eve.

Sierra expected to make adjustments to her life when Latavius came home, but he expected her to bend over backward and be at his beck and call. The plans she had with Marissa and Lane to go out on New Year's Eve were in place long before Latavius showed up. In her opinion, she didn't even stay out that long. The Lyft dropped her off at 2 AM and Latavius was awake and in a foul mood. He was not interested in making love, playing games, or anything else. He picked a fight for no reason, forcing her to concede that she chose friends over him. Latavius was so caught up in his feelings, he accused Sierra of sneaking out with Theo. Latavius slept on the couch and Sierra cried into her pillow until she fell asleep the next morning but she was pleased to find Latavius in her bed when she woke up. She crawled on top of him and they made love. It wasn't passionate, but it was kind.

Sierra wanted to make it work. Latavius was her dream, and dreams didn't change. She took the semester off from school because she couldn't concentrate, and she wanted to focus on her relationship and her family. Sacrifice was needed. *It was just one semester*, she thought, *she would make it up over the summer*. Sierra thought her mom was wrong; she was not putting her life on hold for a man. She knew Latavius wasn't perfect and made some bad decisions before; still she was confident that his street life was in the past. She was his future. There was a lot to process with him being home, and he needed help to get back on his feet. The time off from school freed her up to work extra shifts at Daylight Dreams, and it was helping their home life. She, Latavius and Jordan had movie nights and game time together, and it felt like they were doing okay. They still loved each other.

Latavius was drying the dishes and putting them away when Sierra walked into the kitchen and gave him an awkward peck on the cheek.

"Hey Bae, any luck with the job postings?" Sierra asked.

Latavius turned from placing a dish in the cabinet. "For real, Sea, that's the first thing out of your mouth?"

"Why are you being so defensive? You're the one whose been cleaning all day and trying to avoid me. I'm just making friendly conversation."

"I'm not avoiding you, Bae," Latavius answered. "I'm doing my part. I thought you might be tired after handling Lil' man and putting him down for his nap. Give me some credit. Damn."

"Okay, okay. Wow, it's like everything I say to you is wrong."

"Sea, I'm trying to get a job. You know I'm frustrated. People not trying to hire a convict fresh out of prison. I put enough pressure on myself. I don't need to hear it from you too," he sighed. "How do you think I feel not providing for my family, my only son, and living off of you, in your mama's house?"

Sierra walked over to Latavius and put her arms around his waist and looked up at him. She felt guilty for bringing up work, but money was tight and providing for another adult wasn't cheap. *Love did not cover the late notices.* "I know you're trying and it's not like that. We're a unit. Okay?"

Latavius reached down and kissed her. He loved Sierra so much, but the situation frustrated him. He felt emasculated and not hustling to provide was new, and he didn't like it. He couldn't buy a damn hamburger without going to Sierra. He promised her he would not go back to prison. He would not violate his parole, but he needed money. His manhood was on the line. He was so desperate he would take any legit job. Latavius had been strong, even when his mom tried to give him some work. He avoided his boys, trying to get him back out in the streets, but he was fully aware he was missing out on real bank and Sierra had expensive taste. It was within reason, but still not cheap. It didn't help that punk ass Theo was always coming around. Latavius suspected he gave Sierra money. *Like they were a damn charity case.* Something had to change. Quickly. "You, my ride or die, Bae. That's why I love you. But you best believe I'll be spoiling your bratty ass soon. I'm making it all up to you. Watch me."

"Latavius, I don't like it when you talk like that. Well, spoiling me, I do like that, a lot," Sierra laughed. "But I don't want you back out there. If you're caught with anything, even a dime bag of weed, they're revoking your parole, or at least that's what you told me. I still don't honestly understand how you got out, but you should be just as afraid of the consequences too. I don't want to lose you again. I can't do it Latavius. I can't. I swear. I can't, Bae."

"Sea, calm down, I'm not going back in. All I know is Michael told me I was getting out on early release, and I didn't ask no questions. I just got the hell out of there as soon as they let me. I'm not going back to that life. I told you that. Ima square up like your boy, Theo," he teased.

Sierra gave Latavius a friendly shove, "Shut up," and softly hit him on the head with the kitchen towel.

"Speaking of Theo, I asked him to come by later today." Sierra saw that Latavius shrugged before she finished her sentence. "It's just for an hour or two. I have some design ideas and he helps me with the marketing and business pieces. Besides, he hasn't seen Jordy in a while and Jordy has been asking about Uncle Theo." Sierra looked down at the floor. She did not want another argument, but Latavius needed to understand that Theo was a part of their lives.

"Sea, this is some bullshit. I'm Jordan's dad, not Theo! I can't believe you would keep bringing him here knowing that he wants you. It's disrespectful as fuck."

"That's not true, Latavius! He's my friend. Like a brother." She could hear the lie in her own trembling voice.

Latavius put his hands behind the back of his head. "I'm not even doing this with you. Ima chill at my mama's. I need some air." He was already walking to get his coat and was slipping on the Timbs his mom bought him for Christmas.

Sierra ran after him. "Latavius, wait. How are you even getting there? It's freezing outside."

"Not your concern, Sea." The door slammed

behind him.

Sierra couldn't fight back her tears. Her perfect world was slipping away, and she was helpless to stop it.

11

"Mama, I don't know why you thought it was cool to drag me out in this cold for Debbie's latest food obsession," Charmaine said to Shandra, as she *sampled* on grapes.

"Charmaine, you have three kids at home. It wouldn't hurt you to do a Whole Foods run every once in a while." Shandra smacked Charmaine's hand when she went to pick up more juicy grapes, the green ones this time. "Stop that. It's not sampling when you eat a pound. That's called thievery. Be good. Quit showing out, now."

"Mama. They can afford to lose a few grapes with these crazy prices, and I'm hungry. You rushed me out the house so fast, I didn't have lunch. Thank goodness Eddie was home, so I didn't have to bring my brats, or you would have been on your own."

Shandra was getting impatient with her eldest child. "Quit yapping so much and help me find this vegan pizza." Charmaine cut her eyes toward her mom. "Don't start with me, girl. I'm trying to be a good wife and I'm getting older now. Nothing wrong with being healthy and I promised Debbie I would try."

"So y'all going vegan after Thanksgiving?

That's convenient," Charmaine chuckled. "I'm not judging, even though I know that fake cheese tastes like vomit." Shandra glared at her daughter.

"I'm kidding, mama. I'm proud of you for trying so I won't even try to tempt you with the mustard greens, smothered chicken, and corn on the cob I'm making for dinner tonight," Charmaine said as they approached the freezer aisle.

"Evil child," Shandra chuckled.

"Nah. Charmaine's the good one. Too bad she's already locked down," the woman said, rudely interrupting their mother-daughter teasing.

"Eve. What a pleasure," Shandra said icily.

"Hi Miss Eve. How are you?" Charmaine said, greeting her nephew's grandmother.

"I'm doing quite lovely," Eve answered.

"Eve, what are you doing here?" Shandra suspiciously said.

"Don't show yourself now, Shandra. What are you saying?" Eve moved her head from side to side and waved her hand in the air for additional effect. "I'm not good enough to come over here and shop at this snooty ass store. Even us hood folks like fresh food. But I guess you've forgotten that now that you've moved away with your..*woman*."

"You mean, my *wife*. Shop wherever you want to Eve. That's not my concern. I'm getting quality time in with my daughter and I'd like to get back to-."

"Hold on, now. How's my grandson?" Eve asked. "I haven't seen him since Latavius got home."

"Speaking of Latavius, how exactly did he get to come home, Eve?" Shandra didn't attempt to hide her implications.

"You know exactly how he came home. It's

called early release, Shandra. He's a good boy, and they let him out. He kept telling Sierra that, but she still doesn't believe in him. That's what's holding him back from getting work now. Always trying to prove himself to that girl."

"That *girl* is my daughter, and she is an independent, hard-working woman who-"

Charmaine was visibly uncomfortable, and she knew her mama was on the verge of reaching out and touching this lady. "Miss Eve, we are all so glad that Latavius got an early release. It's good for Jordan to have his daddy home. It's obvious how happy you are and we're happy for you," Charmaine interjected, before a senior citizen fight broke out in aisle three.

Eve's face transformed quickly and lit up with a smile. "Yes, baby, my son is home! Thank you, Jesus! You're right baby girl. I couldn't be happier. As a matter of fact, he's coming over today, so I thought I'd pick up a few things. He might even bring my grandbaby. They could both use a good home-cooked meal." Shandra was fully aware of Eve's shade.

"We're preparing for dinner too. Well, nice seeing you, Miss Eve. Take care and tell Latavius we said hello," Charmaine easily diffused tense situations. Being a high school teacher taught her a few tricks.

"Take care. Hug those beautiful babies for me, Charmaine," Eve replied.

"Eve," Shandra weakly choked out and nodded, as they went in opposite directions.

"Charmaine, I do not need you fighting my battles for me. How would you feel if somebody was talking about your babies like that?" Shandra protested.

"They won't mama. Like you said, they're

babies. No one's talking about them. Besides, Miss Eve is not worth it. You can't take her seriously. She's probably dipping into her own sauce. I don't know why you let her get under your skin."

"Easy for you to say since she thinks you walk on the moon." Shandra was still upset.

"Everybody loves me, mama. I can't help that. I was born a natural charmer," Charmaine smiled.

"Mmm. Hmm. That woman irks my nerves. Like she gives a damn about seeing Jordan."

"Mama, come on. Miss Eve is not ruining our day, and I know you don't want to deal with Debbie's mouth if we don't find this pizza. Ooh, free samples!" Charmaine took off and Shandra followed her, giggling and enjoying each moment with her child. But she had a pestering thought in the back of her mind that she could not shake. Something wasn't right about Latavius coming home so suddenly. She could feel it in her gut.

***

Eve was glad she ran into the Jackson women. She loved messing with Shandra, even if she could never break her. Sierra was just like her mama, nose in the air, and she thought her ass didn't stink. *Skinny heifer.* Charmaine was a sweet girl. She was real and not that much older than Theo. Too bad she was tied down with all those damn kids. Latavius could do so much better than Sierra. That girl had him looking for minimum wage jobs when he could be making real money-for himself and Jordan, and it wouldn't hurt him to help his mama out. She wasn't moving weight like she once did. She was getting too old for this shit, but Latavius had a lot of good years left. He needed to be careful, but he could get back in the game and make his mama proud if he wasn't stuck under that stupid bitch, Sierra. That girl had every excuse in the world for not visiting him in prison. But Shameka made time. She always found a way.

Latavius didn't appreciate Shameka as he should have. Shameka was somebody who would support the real Latavius. Let him be the man he was meant to be and she could handle Jordan. Sierra was raising him to be too soft. Eve could see it every time she looked at the boy. He was always running up under Shandra. No weak men would be in her family, and that meant no weak women. Latavius would see the truth one day; that he needed to drop Sierra, fast. Mama was ready to give him the nudge he needed.

12

Latavius regretted not layering up more. The cold was biting him, and his ears quickly changed from brown to bright pink. He couldn't withstand another moment with Sierra. He loved that girl, but damn, she knew how to push him. Latavius still had visions of Sierra and Theo hugged up the night he came home. He couldn't get them out of his head. Sierra wanted him to believe they were just friends, and that Theo wasn't interested in her like that. But he knew what he saw. His face met Theo's as soon as the door opened. Sierra's back was to him, but he saw the look in Theo's eyes. He saw how Theo had his hands just an inch too low on his woman's waist and how Theo held on a few seconds too long. That man wanted his girl. He was certain of it. He had damn near moved in, trying to be fake daddy and play house with his family. If Latavius didn't know any better, he would think Theo wasn't alone in his lust. Sierra liked the attention. She was a good girl, but all women had their moments. At 30-years-old and after serving two years in a maximum-security prison, he was not interested in playing games. Enough time had been wasted. Latavius was trying to make it work. Jordan deserved that much, but Latavius could barely look at Sierra's ass at times. He saw how her face lit up whenever she mentioned Theo's name; she was nervous about bringing him up, that much was obvious, but she couldn't hide the joy she got from talking about that man. He had been away too long. Sierra always told him how much she missed him and making love to him, but he knew he wasn't pleasing her. Latavius knew her body well, better than his own, and she wasn't reaching the same heights she once did. Sierra didn't pulsate and cream over him like she used to. He knew how his baby felt when he rocked her world and how she always came back enticing him for more, and he was always up for more. Now, he believed she had another man on her mind. He couldn't look at her anymore when they had sex. He was thinking of other women. Former lovers. Women who appreciated him. But he wanted Sierra back, what they had and the life they planned. She was going to be a fancy clothes designer or stylist, and he was going to be an electrician. He could do it if he could just get a job. Then he could go to night school. He knew he had to stay strong. Somebody had to hire him eventually, but his mama told him he had to man up and do what he needed to do. He was too old to be living off a woman. Six weeks was a long time when you were broke.

"Hell Nah, that is him. When they let you out, Tay?" The Lincoln Navigator with the pimped-out rims swerved up to the curb.

Latavius looked over his shoulder and saw the Black Navigator with fully tinted windows. Dre had rolled the front passenger window down. *Fuck*, Latavius thought. He did not have time for Antwan and Dre. Eve told him the other day to stop fucking with them. They were trying to get over on her and couldn't be trusted.

"Dre. Wassup?" Latavius walked over to the truck, sinking his boots in the snow, intensifying the cold as it ripped through him. He peered through the open window. "Twan, what's up man?"

"All good," Twan answered casually.

"Damn, you had like 20 years, what yo' ass doing out?" Dre asked.

"They let a muthafucker out on early release. Shit, I wasn't about to ask no questions."

"For real, even with all the shit, you was into before?" Dre asked.

"Like I said, I didn't ask no questions. I got my Black ass up outta there as soon as I could."

"That's what's up," Antwan chimed in.

Latavius was shivering.

"Man, you out here freezing and shit, get yo' ass in the back seat," Antwan said.

Latavius hesitated. He felt himself getting roped back in.

"Why you standing there looking all scared? Ass turning into a Black bomb pop," Dre laughed.

Latavius opened the door and climbed into the backseat. "It's cold as hell out there. I didn't get out like this in the joint. I forgot how cold it was." The young lady on the other side startled him. "Oh hey shawty, what's up?" She didn't answer. She wore high boots over her knees and a short faux fur coat.

"Where was you going, man? You ain't got no ride?" Dre asked.

"Nah, man. Not yet. I'm still trying to get a job. Trying to go legit. But muthafuckas ain't hiring. I was headed to my mama's house though."

"Yo mama's house? You would've been one frostbitten motherfucker." Dre laughed hard.

Antwan was silent and smoked his blunt without a care in the world.

Latavius was laughing. "This defrost feels good as hell right now, for real dawg. I appreciate you."

Antwan moved the gear out of park and pulled off. "We'll take you to your mama's."

"For real? Thanks, man." Latavius wondered how he ended up riding with Twan and Dre again. He knew he needed to let the ride be the end of it. Fucking with them meant going back to prison or getting shot. One of the two.

Dre was hitting the blunt now and looked back at Latavius. "So Tay. You know we always got work. Fuck that minimum wage shit. They ain't hiring you no way."

"I gotta stay clean, man. I cannot get caught up. I'm not trying to do one more day. Not one."

"Ain't nobody getting caught man. You was doing weak shit with the wrong muthafuckas. We warned you about them but you a man, so you had to do you but this ain't nothing like that." Latavius broke his stare with Dre. "We could use a little help but we ain't desperate. I'm throwing yo' ass a bone. Like you said, you got a little shorty at the house and your girl. I know Sea don't like a broke muthafucker, with her fine chocolate ass."

"Sea's good. You ain't got to worry about that. She got my back. I'll find something. I ain't worried about it," Latavius lied.

"Yo' face tells a whole different story." Dre

was loud and animated as he spoke. "Well, you know how to tap in if you change your mind. We ain't going nowhere."

Dre stretched his right arm behind his seat and put a small plastic pouch in Latavius's hand. Latavius peered down at the package. His heart raced and he could feel sweat breaking through his chilled body. He was filled with nerves, anxiety, and excitement. He knew that feeling well.

"Just a little something to get you through. That's all you." The girl looked over at Latavius but didn't say a word.

"What the fuck you looking at bitch? Mind yo' damn business." Dre snapped.

"Chill out, Dre. It ain't that serious. She cool," Antwan said, defending the young woman.

The girl looked down at her hands and didn't lift her head back up.

***

"Mama, I'm home," Latavius yelled.

"I'll be right down. Hold on," Eve answered. "I got a surprise for you, baby."

Latavius walked to the small kitchen. That aroma pulled him in and he was defenseless. Rotisserie chicken, macaroni, and mashed potatoes with gravy. *What the hell?* He ducked his head into the fridge. *Fruit filled bottled waters?* Latavius thought he was at the wrong house. His mama did not keep fancy water in the fridge, and she was not a cook. Latavius assumed the meal was his surprise. He was tired and hungry and starting digging in. He was loading his plate up when his mom snuck up on him.

"Surprise baby," Eve said, giving a quick hug

to his back.

"Hey mama, this food is-Shameka?"

"She's your surprise!"

"Hey Tay," Shameka waved and smiled at Latavius from across the room.

Latavius stood there with his plate and serving spoon in his hand. His feet weighed him down like heavy cement and his heart was racing. He felt himself slipping away again but didn't know what he was slipping away from. Probably his future. "Shameka, I didn't know you would be here. I uh-"

"Latavius quit being rude. Shameka ain't seen you as a free man in years. Go hug her."

Latavius walked over to Shameka. She was sexy. Her breasts were bigger than they were when she last visited him in prison. She must have had a boob job. But she had that same sweet and sinister smile, and she wore hip-hugging black jeans that wrapped around every inch of her ass. She wore her hair in a short side bob, and she looked like Meagan Good. Latavius embraced Shameka in a wide hug, and she instantly grabbed onto him. She took in his masculine scent and remembered how good his muscles felt against hers. It was a sincere hug, not one of those quick five-second prison hugs.

Eve interrupted. "Latavius let me talk to you for a minute, baby." She led him upstairs into his old room; decorated the same as when he was 17-years-old. Latavius shut the door behind them.

"What's going on, mama?"

"I saw who you rolled up here with."

"Mama, I'm not getting back in with them. I promise. It was just a ride."

Eve grabbed a cigarette from her bosom and

lit it up. She puffed on the cigarette. "You gotta watch those bastards, Latavius. They ain't no good. But that don't mean you can't use them to get back on your feet. Just get in and out, and don't tell them shit about nothing. You gotta keep muthafuckers like that close to your chest. Like enemies." Eve blew out a cloud of smoke and offered the cigarette to her son.

Latavius shook his head no, "I don't smoke no more mama. I don't do nothing. I'm not getting back mixed up with them. I don't know if those muthafuckas set me, Junior, and Roe up. I can't trust them. Especially, Twan. He think he running everything. He ain't shit."

"But Latavius, somebody has to lift you up. They're the last people I want you dealing with but they're connected, even I have to give those assholes a cut. My point is these piss ant jobs don't pay and nobody's offered you an interview. 60 applications, and nothing. I didn't raise you to depend on a woman. You're my son and you need to be a man. Just don't be stupid. Do enough to build up your clientele and maybe help me to-."

"Mama, stop! I'm with Sea now and I need to focus on my family. My freedom. You need to get off my back and what's this bullshit bringing Shameka over here?"

Eve sighed. This was going to be harder than she thought. Her son had toughened up in prison, learned how to say no, even to her. She didn't like it, but she was secretly proud. "Shameka heard you got out, and she came to me." Eve threw her hands up. "I swear on my dead mama. And you know, being your first love and all, I thought it was a good idea. Cheer you up some."

"I'm not a little boy anymore, mama. You need to respect boundaries. That's why I didn't bring Jordan. Chill out. Damn."

"You know what. You're right. Let's go downstairs. You can finish fixing your plate. I worked all day cooking." Latavius looked at her questionably. "I did it for you, baby. I know it's been a while." Eve spent five minutes warming up the pre-made Whole Foods dinner in the microwave. "I can tell Shameka to go home. It's a shame with all that good food, though."

Latavius went to hug his mother. "I love you, mama. She can stay and eat with us but that's it."

***

"I ate way more than I should have. I hope you two liked it."

"It was delicious, Miss Eve. Tasted like my grandma's cooking," Shameka replied.

Eve soaked in the adoration. "Aww. Thank you, baby." Eve let out a fake yawn. "I'm going to lay down. It don't take much to tire out us old folk." Eve wasn't tired, but she needed to give them a chance to get re-acquainted. Latavius saw right through it.

"Alright, mama."

Shameka didn't waste any time. She knew that was her cue. Shameka grabbed Latavius by the arm and walked with him into the living room. She heard Eve's bedroom door shut. Shameka sat on the couch and Latavius joined her. "I know you missed me." Shameka reached over and caressed Latavius in a way that was familiar to him. He immediately grew beneath her hand.

Latavius wanted to deny the pleasure he felt,

but his body had exposed him. He stared at Shameka.

"Shameka, I have a family now. I can't-"

Shameka placed her finger on his lips. "Shhh. I'm not trying to take you away from your family. I just want to make you feel good."

Latavius was breathing hard. He could taste Shameka's finger on his lips. It was sweet, like the dessert he didn't indulge in. Latavius had a flash of Sierra and how he couldn't please her. He thought of how Shameka made him feel in that moment. *Desired.* Shameka took off her shirt and revealed a bouncy new set of breasts. Latavius kept swelling. Shameka unzipped his pants and lowered her head. Latavius made a half-assed attempt to stop her by gently pushing her head back. It wasn't forceful, and she pushed right through it. She swallowed him whole and Latavius leaned back and pushed her head down. Latavius had missed her hot mouth, her luscious tongue, and how much Shameka loved to please him. *Ooh.* He couldn't fight it. He wanted it too bad. *Just this once*, he thought. *Just once.*

13

Sierra breathed a sigh of relief as the last few days went by without any major incident. Latavius had been more attentive. He was spoiling her, tending to her, and he surprised her with a foot massage after a work shift. It was so good; it put her to sleep. Sierra didn't know what sparked the change, but she welcomed it with open arms. She thought it might have been their last fight. Maybe Latavius was just as tired of all the arguing as she was. She hoped he finally believed her, and that there was nothing more than friendship between her and Theo. Sierra tried not to think about her attraction to Theo. She never acted on it and didn't expect that she ever would, not with Latavius around.

Theo's friendship was important, and Sierra didn't want to lose it. She could talk to him about anything, even things she couldn't share with Lane and Marissa. But her family was her priority, and she appreciated that Latavius came home early from prison. It was nothing short of a miracle. If Latavius was willing to work on their relationship and trusted her, she needed to do the same. For a moment she wondered if he had been with someone else. Highly unlikely given how much he was at home looking for jobs and taking care of Jordan, but he did go out at times, more than usual lately. Sierra needed to trust in him. He never gave her reason to doubt him before, and she was genuinely enjoying the peace. She prayed she wasn't about to inadvertently shatter it. She finished styling her hair by bringing baby hairs forward and aligned them perfectly across her forehead and edges with her rattail comb. Time to face the music. *Just get it over with*, she thought. She walked downstairs.

"Damn, baby, you are the finest girl in Detroit. I don't know if I can let you out the house looking that damn good." Latavius looked his girlfriend up and down, and he noticed the peak of cleavage in her almost see-through purple blouse with transparent hues of violent and floral patterns. He twirled Sierra around and checked out her ass. It was small but round. Latavius was smiling ear to ear and kissed his lady, and she kissed him back. It was more friendly than passionate, but it was loving. Latavius gave her ass a gentle squeeze.

"Bae, stop. I mean, squeeze harder," Sierra teased.

"Trying to get me worked up on your way out the door? How much time do we have?" Latavius realized he hadn't made love to Sierra since the incident with Shameka. He regretted it. He was wrong. Thank goodness he didn't have sex with her. He believed that was his saving grace. He let it go too far, but he didn't hit it even though he was so tempted to slide in. Latavius put a stop to their relationship afterward. He texted Shameka that they were done. Whatever they had in the past needed to stay there. He was a gentleman about it. Latavius didn't believe in using women and throwing them away. He thought of himself as a woke type of man and believed he learned all he needed from his mother and sisters. When Shameka called a couple of times, he didn't ghost her, but he believed they came to an understanding. Shameka had a lot to offer a man. He knew some dudes had treated her badly, cheating on her and bullshit like that. Shameka still confided in him and he comforted her, especially when he was in prison. They grew close again, but that was then, and Sierra could never find out-about any of it. Shameka would be okay once she got over their past and young love that once was.

"I wish we could, but Marissa is waiting for me at the conference center. Theo will be here any minute." *There it was. She said it. Theo was picking her up.* He promised to escort her long before Latavius was released, and it wasn't his cup of tea. Marissa and Lane were of course down to go with her but unfortunately, Lane wasn't up for it anymore. He was focused on his family, and Sierra respected that. She fully appreciated how hard it was to keep a family together.

"Theo?" Latavius's face expelled anger, not hurt, just unfiltered anger.

"It's just a ride," Sierra said.

Latavius had already walked away from her. He went to check on Jordan. He could see him from his view, but he felt extra protective at that moment. Sierra followed him.

"Miss me with that, Sea."

"Really? It's just a ride. Latavius you can't get jealous every time Theo comes around. You know we're just friends and this is getting old. Besides, I think he's hooking up with Marissa." Sierra was defensive and annoyed. So much for that patience she practiced for this very moment.

Latavius helped his son with the soft blocks he was playing with. "Every time we get on good terms, that clown coming around. Why he gotta take you? Marissa couldn't give you a ride? I would've paid for an Uber, Lyft, cab, anything but him."

Paid how? Sierra thought but didn't want to go there and risk making things any worse by shaming her man. "Marissa was way on the other side of town. It was just easier to ride with Theo. Latavius, I only get to go because my boss got me tickets. I've been wanting to go to this design show for so many years now. You know how important this is to me."

Latavius shifted his focus back to Sierra. "Everything but your family seems to be important to you. Getting drunk with some snobby rich White people. That's your priority now?"

"Latavius, that's not fair," Sierra barked.

He knew he had hit below the belt. Latavius didn't even understand why he was attacking Sierra. He supported her design dreams. He was proud of her. "I'm sorry, Bae. We shouldn't be arguing in front of Jordan. I just don't like you being alone with Theoretreated. He's thirsty. I can see it."

"My heart is yours. You and Jordy. Y'all are my priority. Period." Sierra bent down to peck Latavius on the lips. In that moment, she silently questioned her decision to go to the show with Theo. Latavius was genuinely hurt. It was all over his face. Sierra kissed Jordan afterward and gave his cheeks a loving squeeze. With perfect timing, the doorbell rang. Sierra stood back up, but Latavius beat her to it.

"I got it." Latavius walked to the door and

opened it. His eyes locked in a standoff with Theo's for about ten seconds before he waved him inside. "Wassup?" Latavius offered as the friendliest greeting he could muster.

"Hey man."

No knife could combat the tension swarming in the air. Suddenly Jordan ran toward the two men.

"Da-da, da-da!" he gleefully screamed as he hugged Theo's knees.

14

It could not have gone worse. Latavius was livid over his son calling Theo da-da, and Sierra failed to calm him down. Theo and Sierra arrived 30 minutes late to the design show. Marissa didn't mind. The men flocked to her, and she enthusiastically entertained them in return. She was a smart woman. She sipped lightly on the champagne. It was a classy event and her friends hadn't arrived, so getting tipsy was out of the question. The real drinks would have to wait.

Theo had waited over an hour in the car while Latavius and Sierra did whatever they were doing. He was patient, but he was freezing in his Range Rover. He was decked out in full winter gear. Long black trench coat, with a matching grey and black scarf and black leather gloves. He rubbed his hands together in a flawed attempt to warm himself. Theo didn't like idly running the engine. He wasn't a fanatic, but he cared about the environment and doing his small part. Uncomfortability was a small price to pay.

Theo was floored when Jordan called him da-da. The kid's timing sucked. Latavius made his feelings about him clear long ago. It showed all over his face how pissed off he was that he was going to the design show with Sierra. Theo thought Latavius had a lot of nerve given he didn't step up. Even as a free man Latavius gave him countless opportunities to be there for Sierra when he wasn't. She deserved better than what Latavius was giving. But Theo was not a homewrecker. If Sierra wanted to be with him, she would need to make a choice and fast. Theo loved her and Jordan, but his patience ran thin. How much more did Sierra need to get a clue?

He sympathized for Latavius-that had to cut him deep to see his son run to another man, full of love and excitement. Theo would be lying to himself if he didn't admit that a small part of his heart smiled at the thought of Jordan's actions tonight. He wished he could see him more, but he respected the boundaries. Even so, he missed that little boy so much. Theo loved Jordan as he would have loved his own son.

***

Sierra sat in Theo's low-lit condo. It looked like a typical bachelor pad, except it was clean and more high-end. Black leather couches and an oversized chair, giant screen television mounted on the wall, Play Stations, and Xboxes-every man's video game dream. Theo had a small bar stocked with bourbon and other whiskeys. He had filled his stainless-steel refrigerator with Surly Darkness, but Sierra found a bottle of Essentia water hiding among the beer. The only food was a leftover box of Szechuan noodles and white rice with a half-gallon of expired milk. Sierra took the Essentia and walked to the sitting area and waited for Theo. He'd gone to his bedroom to change. She let herself sink into the oversized chair. Latavius was angrier than she'd ever seen him before. She was nervous but not fearful; Latavius would never raise a hand to her.

She thought back to what happened before the design show. Sierra hurriedly laid Jordan down for bed. He was exhausted from a full day, but she kept his baby monitor near just in case he woke up. They were loud, but hopefully not so loud that their son would hear them arguing.

"Sea, this shit has got to stop. This joker got my son thinking he's his daddy!"

"He doesn't know any better, Latavius. He's just a baby! You're overreacting."

"I'm overreacting? Okay. That muthafucker wants my family and you ain't doing shit to stop him. I'm starting to think you like this shit. Are you that insecure that you need two men after you? I hate to know what shit was like when I was locked up. I'm too old for these childish ass games, Sea. I'm busting my ass out here hustling, trying to take care of you."

Sierra didn't know what his last comment meant. He was applying for jobs, but it's not like he was working yet. *What the fuck was he talking about?*

"What games? I don't know what the hell you're talking about. You expected me to stop my whole damn life the minute you got home. It don't work like that Latavius. I might be younger than you, but I'm not a fucking child. I've been out here handling my own for a while now if you hadn't noticed. Taking care of your damn son."

"So you do blame me for getting locked up? I knew yo' ass was holding grudges. Now you letting this clown come between us. I thought you was in it for life. Ride or die, huh?" Latavius shook his head.

"I'm still here!"

"Don't *at* me, Sea. I'm not trying to hear it. You can stay here. I'm packing my shit. I need to get outta here. I gotta think."

"So you're abandoning us, again. That's what you do best, right?"

"I'm done with this," Latavius answered.

"Done with what? Me? Our son? This conversation? This family?"

Latavius left Sierra hanging on for an answer and retreated to their bedroom.

***

Sierra didn't enjoy the design show. The entire night was wasted. When she arrived home Latavius was gone, and her mom was watching Jordan.

Sierra's ringtone interrupted her thoughts.

"Sea, are you okay? Mama told me Latavius took off, and she's at your place with Jordan," Charmaine anxiously said.

"I'm not okay, but I will be, eventually." Sierra's voice was flat and Charmaine picked up on it.

"Sis, it'll work out. Just give it time. Where are you? Mama said you weren't even home for five minutes before you took off."

"I'm at Theo's."

"Theo's? Sea don't do anything stupid. I'm a Theo fan, but you're too emotional to be up under him right now. You don't want to be doing something you'll regret."

Sierra was so fed up with being judged, "I'm not fucking him, Charmaine. Damn. How many times do I have to say he's my friend? Latavius is the one who left. Can you just support me tonight without all the lectures?"

Charmaine was concerned, but careful not to push her sister too hard. She knew when she needed to just listen and be there. This was one of those times. "Alright, Sea. You're a big girl. I wasn't trying to imply anything. I care about you. I'm sorry you're going through this."

Sierra sniffled. "Thanks, sis."

"Mama is a different story though," Charmaine said.

Sierra rolled her eyes unbeknownst to her sister. "Really? She didn't give me a hard time tonight. She knew I needed space, but I hate she got dragged into my mess."

"She loves spending time with her grandbabies. She's not worried about tonight. You know she's not crazy about Latavius, anyway." Charmaine saw an opportunity to lighten the mood. "Girl, mama still salty about you not going to the store with us."

"Are you serious? Me and Latavius had got into it. It was just a lot. Wait-is mama still on that vegan kick?" Sierra's tone was lighter, and she was almost smiling.

"Hell Nah, she was over here eating on spaghetti, meatballs, and ribs two days later," Charmaine laughed.

Sierra heard a beep and saw Marissa's name pop up on her phone. "Charmaine, sorry sis. I gotta go. Marissa's calling me. I gotta take this."

"Okay. Stay safe. Love you."

"Love you too."

"Hey, Marissa. You made it home alright?"

"Yeah, girl. I been here for a minute."

"I'm so sorry I was so late after you came out to support me. I just keep messing up with Latavius."

"It's growing pains, Sea. He's been away a lot longer than he's been home. Y'all need some time to get to know each other again, and you're living together for the first time. Be patient. He'll come around."

"Damn, look at you sounding all mature and shit. You might be right."

"Of course, I'm right," Marissa said while refreshing her mascara on her false eyelashes. "Now my turn. Sea, guess who's taking me out tonight?" Marissa asked excitedly.

Sierra appreciated her friend's advice, but she was tired and didn't feel like talking about Marissa's escapades. "Let me guess, another baller?" Sierra condescendingly said. Marissa was free to date who she wanted, but Sierra had genuine problems at the moment.

"Yes, Mamacita! Like they say, if he can't buy a Birkin." Marissa tickled herself with her own comments and failed to pick up on Sierra's poor attitude. Marissa laughed innocently. "It's Derek! You know I had my eye on him for a minute now. Girl, he finally swiped me back, and it's been on ever since. He's taking me to that new restaurant downtown. He got us some type of VIP late reservation, and I've been starving it out all day, even at the design show. It wasn't easy. Those appetizers looked good! Ooh, but he is just so fine. Shit. I hope I can eat in front of him."

"So, what kind of games are you playing, Marissa? It's dude after dude, and now you got Theo all mixed up in this. I won't stand by and let you play with his heart like this."

"Whoa, bitch. Wait, a fucking minute. What does Theo have to do with this and how the fuck is it your business? You wanna bang him or something, Sea? Because I sure as fuck don't."

"Nah, but he's my friend."

"And what the hell am I?"

"You are my friend, my best girlfriend, of course. I love you. I just don't want him getting hurt and you know you go through-"

"Go through what? Men? That's my damn business and how dare you act like I'm out here screwing everybody I date. I don't have any damn kids Sea, and I can live my life how I damn well please. You chose to lock yourself down and now you don't know how to handle that shit. And for the record, ain't nobody tripping over Theo's broke-ass either, but you got a man at home, right? Okay, bitch." Marissa hung up before Sierra could reply. She had a baller waiting for her. Sierra would not ruin her night with her fake-ass, self-imposed life crisis. She let it roll off her shoulder like the silky dress she squeezed into.

***

Theo found Sierra balling into his leather couch. He sat the glass of water down that he'd just fetched for her, noticing that she had a bottle of Essentia. "I don't know what to do," she cried.

Theo sat next to Sierra and he held her close. He was that reliable shoulder. He would serve his role faithfully if that's what Sierra needed. He reached over to his table and handed her a box of Kleenex. Sierra wiped her face and raised her head off Theo's shoulder.

"Theo, I can't be crying to you all the time. It's not right. You do so much as it is, and I definitely can't take any more money. Latavius would go off the rails if he knew."

"I don't think you need to worry about all that right now. What happened?"

"Everything. How am I gonna fix things with Latavius?" Sierra asked wholeheartedly.

Theo ignored the gut punch and remained silent.

"He was already jealous of you. I could tell, but Jordan calling you da-da, it was too much for Latavius."

"I'm sorry, Sea. You know I've never taught him to do anything like that."

Sierra was still sniffling and took a moment to blow her nose. She walked to the bathroom and tossed the dirty tissue into the garbage can and quickly splashed water on her face. When she returned, she continued talking while in mid-thought. "I wasn't trying to say you did, Theo. I know you wouldn't do anything like that. But how am I supposed to control what a two-year-old does? He doesn't even know what he's saying. How is it my fault that Latavius was locked up Jordan's whole life? He is blaming me for everything. I don't even know if he loves me anymore. He's gone, Theo. He left me."

Theo looked directly at Sierra. "Do you love him?"

"Huh? What? How could you ask me that? I waited for him."

"Sea, it's a simple question. Do you love Latavius?"

Sierra was uncomfortable, and she stood as she spoke. "I really can't believe you would ask me that. I've stuck by his side this entire time. Whose side are you on, Theo?"

Theo rose off the couch. "I'm tired of these games, Sea. I won't do it anymore. I want you and I think you feel the same."

"Why is everybody accusing me of playing games? I'm not. I'm with Latavius, Theo."

"Nah, Sea, you here with me," Theo said as he leaned in to kiss the woman he'd been yearning for years. He noticed Sierra didn't pull back from him. In fact, she leaned in. Her mouth was sweet and warm and his tongue was hungry. Theo felt the chemistry that had raged through him all this time, come to life. He had waited so long for this moment and he savored it. Theo led Sierra back to the couch and gently laid her down and got on top of her. He lost himself in Sierra. Kissing her, touching her, fondling her, softly.

"Mmm, mmm, ahhh," Sierra moaned. All intelligible thoughts raced from her mind. She knew what love and lust felt like when it came together, and she was all in. This moment, right now. She pulled Theo's shirt off and welcomed his chest as it pressed against hers. Sierra didn't stop him from taking her breasts into his mouth, fully and slowly and teasing her dark, raised nipples. Warmth chased through her body and shivers overtook her. Sierra didn't stop Theo when he unzipped her jeans and touched her in her sacred place. He was the conductor playing her orchestra, and he was hitting every note. She needed to release, so badly. It had been so long. Theo aggressively took in her mouth while massaging her below. She pulsated uncontrollably, wincing with pleasure, softly crying with guilt.

15

"I didn't expect you to be out all night," Shandra said, fully aware of her implications. Jordan was giggling and eating eggs off his grandmother's plate.

"Mom. It's way too early for you to be judging me. I'm wiped and I need to get ready for work." Sierra gave Jordan a big hug and wiped his mouth off. He was already dressed and ready for the day.

Shandra took a sip of her caramel cappuccino and took a bite of her turkey bacon. "What you know about judgment? Child, please. I like Theo. You could do a lot worse. Just don't forget to make up your own bed before jumping in another one."

"Mom stop it. Are you gonna keep Jordy for me today? Unless you know where Latavius is because I don't have a clue."

"In the streets, I imagine." Shandra was on a roll. She woke up feisty this morning. "I can take my baby for the day. He hasn't had quality time with his grandma Debbie fog testin a while because his mama doesn't visit like she's supposed to."

Sierra ignored her mom's shade. "Thank you, mom, and for the ride, I need you to give me." She hugged her mom. "I need to take a quick shower and get ready." As Sierra ran upstairs, she yelled back to her mother, "Hey, mom. How's that vegan life going?"

"Ha. Ha. Ha. Now who's judging?" Shandra shot back, tickled that her daughter made fun of her. Shandra knew her good spirits were because Sierra was ridding herself of Latavius, or so she hoped. Shandra had no ill will toward the man and believed he was a decent father, but he came with heavy baggage. That street life would always be a part of him. Because of it, there would always be trouble brewing. Her gut didn't lie.

***

This was one of those moments when Sierra appreciated who she was. Her clothes for the day greeted her, they were wrinkle-free and hanged. She'd prepared her outfits carefully a week in advance; it was a habit at this point, and she enjoyed it. It gave her peace, creating beauty. She looked at her Fitbit and saw she had time for her call. She made countless mistakes last night and needed to fix one of them right now.

"Marissa don't hang up. I was out of my mind last night. That whole conversation was on me. I'm so, so sorry."

Marissa didn't respond. She wasn't angry but wanted more groveling.

"Fine. You are the best bestie in the world, and I wish I could be as fabulous as you," Sierra pleaded.

"Not in this life, but you can try for the next one," Marissa giggled.

"I can't believe you make me say that every

time we fight. My consistent bestie."

"Consistent. That's new. I like it!" Marissa laughed. "We're okay. I know last night was crazy with all the drama with you and Latavius. You get a pass."

"You're being easy on me. I feel terrible, about so much. I know I've been a bad friend, always focused on me."

"Sea, it's okay, honestly. And I know you gotta do what you gotta do with Latavius, but if I'm being honest, and you know I am because I don't bite my tongue, you've always belonged with Theo. That might not be my place to say, but it's how I feel. That man is always talking about you. And trust there is NO chemistry between me and Theo, so don't ever let that slip in your hard head again, girl."

Marissa had no idea how relieved Sierra felt to hear that. The guilt of betraying Latavius weighed her down, but if Marissa wanted Theo, she didn't know how she would ever forgive herself. It was so peaceful staying overnight with Theo. She slept in his bed, fully clothed, but he held her all night and she slept like she hadn't in a long time. Theo was easy. *Was that how love felt?*

"I don't deserve you." *He always talks about me?* Sierra's heart warmed.

"This is true. But seriously, I think we're all stressed. You with Latavius, Lane with Damont, and I feel like I don't even know who I am."

"A good ass-woman, that's who you are," Sierra said firmly in support of her friend.

"Yeah, I hear you. I'm getting so tired of these dudes. They get too attached."

"Guess I don't have that problem. Latavius

didn't even come home." Sierra pouted. "No texts. I don't know where he is."

"He'll be back. Trust. But you know what? The trio needs to get some self-care time in. Let's do something soon. Lane could definitely use the support. I'm worried about him."

"I am so down. I'll talk to my mom and Charmaine. See if one of them can watch Jordy in the next couple of days."

"Kiss him for Auntie Rissa. Talk later. Smooches."

"Damn it!" Sierra yelled at herself. She was running late.

***

Tremaine lived with his mom in a small apartment, but he'd never forgot the Sojourner Truth projects he grew up in. Latavius was his closest childhood friend. They hadn't seen each other since Latavius got out. Tremaine was busy with his hustle, and Latavius was trying to find his way back into the real world. Tremaine was lucky. He'd never served a day in jail. He kept his business, his.

It wasn't even a question when Latavius showed up. He was Tremaine's boy, and he was welcome in his home. Latavius crashed on the couch.

"Man, I appreciate you letting me stay here last night. I had to get away." Latavius was wearing yesterday's clothes.

"For sho. You know moms crazy about you."

Latavius smiled. "I appreciate her. Sorry about ya' pops, man. I know that was rough."

Tremaine's father succumbed to a heart attack a year ago. "It's alright. Me and moms getting through. But she stay busy, man," Tremaine chuckled. "I mean, she never sits down. She's at the grocery store now. When she found out you came, she got to talking about making a big dinner tonight. So you gotta stay."

"Bet. That's what's up."

Tremaine looked down at his black cell phone. It was buzzing. "Hold up, man. Dre's outside."

"Dre?" *What's he doing here?* Latavius thought.

Tremaine unlocked the triple bolted door and let Dre inside.

It surprised Latavius to see him. *When did Tremaine start hanging with Dre? He was always low key.*

"Damn, man. Rough night?" Dre said looking at Latavius. Dre sat down on the sofa across from him.

"Something like that man."

Tremaine jumped into the conversation. "I was trying to tell you Dre was stopping by."

Latavius silently disagreed.

"How's the job hunt going? You hit the big time yet?" Dre said sarcastically.

"I'm still looking. Something will turn up. I'm handling it," Latavius answered.

"That package come in handy?"

Tremaine was confused, but he wasn't trying to get too deep in their business.

Latavius didn't want to admit that he sold the glass, but he needed things as a man and was building up savings for him and Sierra. They needed some wheels, bad. "I owe you, man. That's it though. As I said, I'm going legit. I have some interviews next week," Latavius lied. "I ain't too worried."

Tremaine chimed in. "That's good, Tay. It'll happen for you."

Dre hopped back in the conversation. "That's cool, man. I respect a man taking care of his family. These hoes and babies ain't cheap," Dre laughed. He didn't notice he was laughing alone. "I got a proposition for you, Tay, and like I said, I ain't trying to interfere with you getting out the game, but I need to cash in on that favor."

Latavius straightened up and suspiciously eyed Dre.

"One and done. Real quick. I wouldn't even come to you, but I need somebody I can trust. When shit is this important, you just can't trust some of these muthafuckers. But you the real deal. Scratch each other's back, right? Few stacks in it for you. Hold you over until you working."

"I don't know Dre. I'm not trying to get locked back up. My girl would kill me. And I gotta kid. I'm not trying to be some Black absentee father. I love my son."

"I love my sons too. All five of them bastards." Dre cracked himself up more than anyone else. "This is for your family, but you got street family too. Don't forget who's looked out for you. Me and Twan put you on the grind when you didn't know shit but that baby grind yo' mama had going." Dre could see that Latavius wasn't convinced. "You ain't even gotta deal with no weight, man. Just be the lookout. Nothing more."

"Latavius, this might be a good opportunity for you. Help you get back on your feet. Take off some pressure," Tremaine added.

Latavius's hair stood up on his back. *Tremaine*

was with this bullshit? Fuck! He needed the money, and he was indebted to Dre's crazy ass. If he didn't do it, he would be done. Maybe it wasn't that bad. He'd be a lookout, and then this shit was done for real. Sierra could never find out. He already fucked up with Shameka, but she would be done with his ass if she knew he was risking his freedom, their future. That's if they still had one.

Dre wasn't done. "Latavius, damn man. It ain't like you gone be on a corner slangin' like some rookie."

"This is it, man. I'm in and I'm out. No licks, right?"

"Nah, nothing like that. But you never know what muthafuckas might try to pull." Dre reached in his pants. "Take this. You gotta be strapped. Courtesy of Twan."

Latavius took the 9 mm. He had no choice.

***

DETROIT, 2002

"And hurry up boy, I ain't got all day."

Latavius walked to the kitchen and retrieved a pre-filled plastic bag. It was already tied. He put the money in the makeshift safe that sat on top of the counter.

"Quit all that fussing, James. I hate to have to cut you off, but you know I will," Eve said defending her son.

James stood outside the storm door eagerly awaiting his next hit. "It's my nerves, Eve. Forgive me. I didn't mean no harm."

"Mmm. Hmm," Eve said, smoking her

cigarette. She had no qualms with Latavius getting familiar with the game. He'd be a man one day and needed to be prepared to hustle. He was 12-years-old and learned quickly. Her girls were two divas-uninterested and running after boys. They weren't built like her. She had very little patience for them, and the feeling was mutual on their end.

Latavius walked back over to James. He opened the storm door and placed the small plastic package in the man's hand. James snatched it and quickly raced from the porch.

"Dope fiends. Hmm. Never fuck with your own product, baby. That sauce ain't worth it. I know it."

"That's why you left daddy, right?"

"Yeah, like I told you, a million times. I was in love with Sam with my whole heart." Eve reminisced about a time she treasured. "He was one of the biggest dealers around. Ooh, how I miss those days. But he messed up and started using. Life was so good before that, but after he got hooked on that stuff, he wasn't the same. Couldn't have nobody like that around my babies."

"Don't you miss him? Is he ever coming back home?" Latavius innocently asked.

"I did miss your daddy-before he got hooked. I don't think we'll ever see him again, baby. Last I heard, he was somewhere in San Bernardino. Probably dead by now." Eve made the callous statement with no consideration that she was speaking to a child.

That's all Latavius knew of his dad. He barely remembered him. In his mind, he was dead before he met him. According to his mom, the best thing he taught her was how to hustle. It allowed her to provide for her kids and not depend on a man. Eve had men, but she controlled the relationships. Latavius wondered what it was like when his parents were together. His mom still professed about how she loved his dad, but he never saw her in love, at least what he understood of it. She treated men more like a business opportunity. She always focused on what they could do for her and when they had no more to give, she was done. Most men couldn't handle a woman selling her own product. Eve intimidated many of them. They had no issue with the lifestyle, but it was a man's job. They felt emasculated. It didn't bother her. She refused to compromise herself. She wasn't big time and didn't want to be. Eve did enough for her and her family to live comfortably. Her cut to the local guys was low, thanks to Sam. His reputation carried over to her and she got decent protection in return. Nobody fucked with her.

"Latavius, close and lock that door and help me count this money."

"Yes, ma'am."

"You polish that 32 like I asked?"

"Yep."

"Good."

Guns didn't scare Latavius. He was used to handling them and counting thousands of dollars. As a young boy, he didn't judge his mother. He didn't know of a time when they weren't selling drugs or bootlegging beer, vodka, and whiskey. What he knew was to keep his mouth shut. He told the kids at school that his mom was a daycare teacher and sold tabs at a local bar. That was the line Eve taught him and his sisters to say. It wasn't a total lie. Eve volunteered occasionally and covered for her girlfriends, who worked at the neighborhood childcare center when they were short-staffed. Eve told Latavius she enjoyed selling tabs, but that job was only a few hours of work each week. Helping his mom with her low-key distribution was a way of life. Eve taught him not to be afraid of jail. It was part of the life. All men did a little time here and there. It would strengthen him in the long run. Latavius loved his mother and knew as the man of the house he needed to be there for her. He felt special, but he was well aware he was being robbed of his childhood.

"Uh-mama. Can I go play football with Tremaine after we finishing counting? I did everything you said. I even cleaned my room. Please, mommy. Please."

"Latavius, I saw that room. Clean ain't the word, but you gone have to catch up with Tremaine another time. You know tomorrow is payday for a lot of these fools and we got work to do. I can't do it by myself."

"Just for one hour, please."

"The clothes you wearing, those Nike Air Trainers you wearing, and that dirt bike you ride didn't pay for they damn selves. You kids just want more and more. Let me tell you, baby, ain't no free handouts in life. You want to keep getting nice things you need to learn to hustle. Your daddy ain't around, so I gotta teach you how to be a man. Now sit yo' little ass down and help me finish counting this money so we can start cutting. It's gone be a high traffic day tomorrow."

Latavius did as he was told. He sulked the entire night and countless others that followed. Life was a bitch.

16

"I'm not looking for a pity party, but you can dote over me."

Marissa and Sierra smothered him in hugs, right there on the floor. "Okay, okay. I love you too now get off me, bishes."

They made Lane smile. "My work here is done. If all you needed was two fine ass women to crawl over you Lane, you should've said something a long time ago," Marissa teased.

"In your dreams, mama."

"I do like dreaming," she winked at Lane.

"Eww. Y'all so nasty. Stop it." Sierra said. "Lane, we got all your favorite food, your fancy bourbon, everything, and by the way Damont is the biggest fool on earth. What happened? Tell us everything."

Marissa affectionately snuggled up next to Lane and rested her head on his shoulder.

"Well, you know we've been having problems for a while, but it was always Damont who didn't trust me. I was the fool and the faithful one. I should have known based on the way we started out."

"Don't blame yourself. Believing in the love

you thought you had is not wrong," Sierra said.

Lane nodded his head but wasn't sure he agreed with Sierra. "He took the kids and went to his mother's. At least that's what he told me. I know he's with Thomas. I'm not a fool. It's over."

Ruby came rushing in. "Ahh, come here girl." Lane rubbed Ruby's golden-brown hair. The golden retriever was panting and loving the attention. The girls joined in on the doggy love, rubbing their fingers in her hair and snuggling close to Ruby. The dog sucked up the love and laid down at the feet of the three friends. Lane continued petting Ruby. "Damont hates pets. Allergies. Whatever. So I get to keep my baby Ruby," he said with pride. "But my other babies are gone. I don't know what to do."

"Did Damont actually say he was done? That he wants a divorce? Marissa asked. "Don't assume the worst, Lane."

Lane wiped his face with tissues. "He said he needed time. Everybody knows that's code for divorce. Two years and he's already gone. How is it that I was more committed than he was?"

Sierra subconsciously sucked air between her teeth. A pang of guilt swept over her as she thought about the mistake she made with Theo. But it didn't feel like a mistake to her; it felt good, but she knew it was wrong because she loved Latavius.

"Something I said?" Lane asked.

"No, sorry. Stomach cramps. My period is probably coming soon. Lane, I don't want you giving up. You have to fight if you want your man. Look at me and Latavius. He hasn't been home for days, and he finally texted me today. I thought he was gone for good."

"What? He texted you?" Marissa asked. "I didn't want to say anything, but I thought he was out. What did he say, Sea?"

"It's not long, but you'll get the point." Sierra read the text message.

Bae, let's talk. I know I fucked up. I love you. I'm coming home.

"Is that all it takes for him to get you back? You an easy bitch. You better make him grovel. Staying out all those nights, no communication for days, you don't know who he might be fucking with?" Marissa asserted.

Sierra's cramp returned. *Latavius wouldn't cheat.* Sierra believed he was stronger than she was, a better person. *He was at Tremaine's, not worried about some nasty ass hoochies.* She imagined the word *guilty* was painted across her forehead in bright red with all caps. She busied herself with a bag of Ruffles she purchased. She damn-near emptied the store of all its junk food earlier that afternoon. Sierra had to make up the store trip with Shandra; her mom wouldn't let it go. Sierra enjoyed spending time with her mom, and it was fun today since the vegan phase was over, so there was a lull before Debbie's next health craze would kick in.

Shandra always covered Sierra's bill. Sierra accepted it but she felt bad because she wasn't self-sufficient. She looked forward to the day when she could spoil her mom. Designs and styling would make it happen; one day, she was certain. Shandra let her know once again, exactly how she felt about Latavius. In her opinion, Latavius was bringing Sierra down. He made her drop out of college and he was still out in the streets. Shandra had not patience for Latavius and wanted him out of her daughter's life. Sierra reminded her mom that putting a pause on school was her decision and to allow her work things out with Latavius, herself. Shandra let it go for the time being.

Sierra crunched into her chips. They steadied her temperamental nerves.

"Everybody knows Sea and Theo will end up together. But can we stop with her soap opera now and get back to me?" Lane demanded.

"Hold up-I have real issues too. I'm more than just a sexy shoulder to cry on." Marissa exclaimed.

"What's wrong?" Lane and Sea said in unison.

"Nothing, I just-I'm going to Puerto Rico. I've been talking to my aunt over there. I need to find myself, figure out my life."

"Look at you being mature. I'm proud of you girl and if you need a travel companion, my schedule just freed up." Lane said, emphasizing the empty home that sat in the town of Plymouth. It was beautiful and fit well in the upscale neighborhood. The interior-styled with modern-contemporary elements, was warm and familial. Lane had a way of making everything feel like home. "It's been a long winter. My tan needs refreshing."

"I'm happy for you, Marissa. And I too can free up my schedule anytime. I'm willing to make that sacrifice for you," Sierra chuckled.

"Thank you, jerks, but I'm doing this one solo. I'll let you know everything, when I'm leaving and how long I expect to be there, but I won't rush my time there." Marissa was petting Ruby and staring at nothing in particular.

They stayed at Lane's for hours, reminiscing

and reassuring Lane that he was the *catch* in his marriage. They would be there no matter what, even if Damont wasn't. They were cleaning up the mess they made. Wrappers, glasses, and plastic bottles surrounded them. Afterward, they gathered around Lane's fireplace. He made them all some Ghirardelli hot cocoa. Lane appreciated feeling needed, and the women welcomed the attentiveness.

Sierra received a text from Latavius, *I love you, baby. I can't wait to see you.*

Sierra's heart danced. One word from Latavius and she melted. She felt good. Real good. "I love Latavius so much. I hope you and Damont can reconcile."

"Thanks, Sea, time will tell." Lane was nervous, and he flicked his fingers. He looked at Sierra, "I need to tell you something."

"Lane, what's wrong? You look like somebody died," Sierra said.

"Sierra. Please."

Sierra repositioned herself and sat upright, "Ok Lane, this is a lot of drama, even for you. What's the deal?" Sierra braced herself for bad news. She knew Lane well enough to know that whatever it was, it was important.

"I'm being serious, Sea. No joking. Damont told me something disturbing about Latavius." Sierra continued looking at Lane. "Sea, you have to promise me you won't say anything to anyone. I mean it. This is something I feel you need to know, but Damont could lose his law license. He made me swear on everything that I wouldn't tell you. He's an ass, but I don't want him broke because that would make me broke," Lane said in an obvious attempt at levity.

"Alright, bruh. Whatever. But you're scaring me. Just spit it out."

"I know why Latavius couldn't get out before. I know what he got into as a kid."

"Lane, I know he got into trouble. He told me himself, but it wasn't a big deal. Whatever Damont told you must be wrong. If you're trying to drag Latavius's name through the mud, I'm not having it."

Lane knew Sierra was scared. He was dealing with too much with his own family to take it personally. "Sea, he shot somebody."

Sierra gasped and shook her head no.

"Wait. I meant that's what Latavius said. He took a rap for somebody, but it's on *his* record that he shot someone."

Sierra was up and pacing. "I'm not following Lane. I don't understand what you're saying."

Marissa spoke up. "Sea, it's okay. Just try to relax."

"So you know already? I'm the last. He's just my child's father and my man but okay."

"No, I don't know anything. I'm just trying to be supportive," Marissa insisted.

Lane took control of the conversation. "All I know is something went down. I don't know everything but Latavius and a friend, um, Jerome, Jermaine-"

"Tremaine?"

"Yeah, that's his name. They walked up on something they weren't supposed to see. A robbery, I think. I guess there was a scuffle and Tremaine killed a man. I don't know if it was intentional, to kill him, but for whatever reason Latavius took the rap."

"What? Why would he do that? Are you

saying my child's father, the love of my life, has a murder on his record?"

"No, no, no. He was a kid. He got a deal because there was a self-defense claim and his attorney took the offer. I'm not telling you just to be gossiping. I'm telling you because he would have never got out on early release with something like that on his record."

"Except he did, so what you're saying can't be true, right?"

"I'm gonna be straight with you, Sea. Damont said there's no way in hell he got out without giving somebody else up."

"You mean he snitched?" Marissa gasped. "Oh, shit." She took a long swallow of her hot cocoa.

"Is that what Damont said?" Sierra asked, not wanting to hear the answer.

"I'm so sorry, Sea." Lane put his around Sierra's shoulder. "Now, don't you go assuming the worst. I'm not saying he did, or he didn't, but it doesn't look good."

"How does Damont know? He's never worked on Latavius's case."

"Lawyers run in small circles. Damont didn't cut his criminal law ties when he switched over to family law." Lane paused and took a deep breath. "To be honest, Damont was looking out for me. He knows we're close, and it raised red flags for him when Latavius got out early. It scared him. At least, that's what he told me. I don't have any reason not to believe him. Well, besides him being a cheating ass liar."

Something was off, Sierra thought. Damont had mixed information, or he didn't understand clearly.

One of the two. She knew Latavius. He would never snitch. If he took the rap for Tremaine. *Why would he start snitching now?*

"Something about this doesn't sound right. I'll get to the bottom of it, though. Later. But now, I could use a real drink. Give me some of that over-priced bourbon." Sierra suppressed her fears. She didn't have the courage to face them.

Marissa and Lane looked at one another and laughed out loud.

"Well, hot damn!" Lane exclaimed. "Get this bish a bourbon!"

17

"I already paid you young muthafuckas. I know I don't owe you shit."

"Whoa. Simmer down, Miss Eve. You good, but we businessmen, right?" He waited until she nodded in agreement. "We have to keep up with inflation, cost of living, etcetera, etcetera. You a businesswoman, you know how it is," Dre said, sucking on his purple Tootsie Roll Blow Pop.

"I won't be good for long with the way y'all collecting."

Antwan commanded the room, even before he spoke. "Miss Eve. We provide you good protection. Things change. If it wasn't for us, you wouldn't be able to do what you do. Someone would've taken you out a long time ago. You here because I allow you to be here."

Antwan was one of the biggest dealers in Detroit. He was unique. He knew how to control money and not let it control him, and he was smart enough to keep a lower profile than other dealers. His sole focus was on business. He believed in action over words and only spoke when reinforcement was necessary. He made himself comfortable in an old rocking chair Eve kept from her grandmother. He wasn't a man who waited for invitations. He claimed territories as he saw fit.

Eve continued standing, her nerves were on full display. She silently prayed that they would not see her safe. *Since when did they just drop in without warning? This was bullshit. They had an honor system.* She couldn't stand all these young wanna be thugs.

Dre walked over to Eve. He stood within an inch of her face. He could feel Eve's heavy breath. "Relax, Miss Eve. I got you." Dre touched Eve, slowly, fondling her shoulder with his long fingers. He made his way to her neck and finally to her bra. He placed his icy hand inside and scooped up Eve's right breast, slowly massaging her without breaking his gaze. Dre brought his hand back up and quickly grazed Eve's chin with his cold finger. He leaned in an inch closer and licked her closed lips, once, from bottom to top. "For an old ass broad, your titties still soft. You taste good too."

Eve was shaken. She wanted to break his fucking neck. *Punk ass boy. So ungrateful.*

Dre flipped through the wad of cash he removed from Eve's bra. "This should do it. For now."

Antwan was still sitting. Watching. "Miss. Eve, I been hearing some bothersome things. Things on good authority."

Eve would not let them see her squirm. They could keep that money. She had plenty. Eve couldn't wait to get away from Dre. His gross wet saliva sitting on her lips. Eve wiped her mouth with the back of her hand and gave Dre a look that could have proved fatal. She sat down in a chair and focused on Antwan. His statement bothered her. He was the boss and the person she needed to keep happy. Dre was a clown, hanging on to Antwan's coattails and leftovers. "Antwan, I don't know what you've been hearing, but I'm sure it has nothing to do with me."

Dre chimed in on cue, "It's about your bitch ass son. You better make sure he comes through for us or somebody else gone be coming for him."

Eve looked confused. *Was he threatening her son?*

"Tay been running his mouth. We got word you told him to do it," Antwan accused.

"What? I did not-"

Antwan held his hand up, "This is on good authority, Miss Eve. No point trying to lie. Like my boy said, make sure your boy help us out. It can all stay between us. Family."

"I got enough family," Eve replied with an attitude.

"Miss Eve don't bite the hand that feeds you. We trying to help you. You know what these muthafuckers would do to Tay if they knew he was out here snitchin'? You want a body bag at your door, or you want us, your family, at your door?"

Eve released a loud sigh. She'd planned to get her nails done with her daughters, a rare occasion, but her eldest insisted. *How the hell I go from acrylics to body bags. I have to get out of this life. If only I knew how. Damn you, Sam, all this is your fucking fault.*

Dre walked to the kitchen. He was comfortable. Some small part of him truly believed Latavius was family. He and Eve had been there for him when he was young. Dre was hungry a lot, as a child. His grandma did the best she could with five kids running around but there was never enough food, and Dre was an outcast. Kids made fun of him because he had dark skin, was skinny with big gapped teeth, and was too tall for his age. Dre stood six foot six as an adult. Antwan gave him a chance to come up when everyone else thought he was a joke. He would always be loyal to Antwan. Whatever Eve and Latavius did for him in the past was old news. It was a new day, and he had clout. Dre grabbed a cloudy but clean glass from the peeling wooden cabinet. He passed on, rinsing it with the tap. *Flint and all.* He took the Brita pitcher from the white refrigerator and filled the cloudy glass. Dre took one long swallow and walked back to the small living room with Eve and Antwan. He didn't bother with a coaster. He sat his glass on a ledge next to the stairs after he finished.

"Tay is our family. We all grew up together and looked out. He was always cool, but prison must have changed him. It's almost like you both forgot the rules of the game. If we didn't consider you family, we wouldn't even be having this conversation," Antwan said.

Eve wanted to vomit. This fake jokester was threatening her while at the same time offering her a lifeline. *How did anyone hear her conversation with Latavius? She had whispered. No other visitors were close enough to hear them. She was certain of it. Besides, Latavius didn't agree. Here they were branding her son a snitch on gossip, or maybe they made up the whole damn thing and just wanted to have Latavius under their thumbs.* Eve was all for Latavius hustling again, but she didn't want her son indebted to these two clowns. It was bad enough they owned her, but they couldn't have her son. Latavius had such potential.

"Miss Eve, remember, we were never here. I would hate for Latavius to find out we paid you a visit, today. What that would mean for you, and him? Stay blessed, Miss Eve. I'll tell my mama you send your best." Antwan shut down any opportunity for someone to say more. Dre followed him out the door.

Eve threw Dre's drinking glass at the wall, indenting the home's flimsy drywall and shattering the glass into a thousand pieces.

***

Tremaine received a text from Dre.

You keep an eye on that muthafucker or your ass will be on ice.

Tremaine begrudgingly pressed the thumbs up on his phone. Tremaine wished no harm to his bruh. They went so far back and bailed each other out of shit more times than he could count. Latavius had his back when the childhood mess went down. He owed Latavius but not with his life. The Latavius he knew wouldn't do the shit the streets accused him of doing. But he had been away for a minute. People changed. Tremaine gave him the benefit of the doubt even now, but he wasn't going down for anybody. He already lost his pops. He wasn't one of those little homies running around without a daddy. His pops was the best and had treated his moms like gold. Tremaine was not about to leave her alone. Bruh or not. His loyalty was to his family. He could not be associated with a snitch. Tremaine worked hard to build up his street cred, quietly. He wasn't flashy like Dre's clown ass, but the streets respected him. He damned sure hoped Latavius hadn't bitched out, for his own sake.

18

When can I see you again?
I don't think that's a good idea.
Why not?
What happened the other night wasn't okay.
We didn't cross any lines.
Yes, we did.
When we cross lines you'll know, trust me.
I'm serious.
Me too. I love you and not as your friend. I want you.
We can't do this Theo. It's not right.
Is that fool back?
Latavius is coming home. I love him. He's my family.
You know what we had. That was special. It was
real. You wouldn't have responded to me the way you
did if you truly loved him. I felt the love you have for
me. I didn't imagine that.
I can't be with you. I owe it to Latavius to try for our
family.
I might not be here to catch you next time, Sea. I love
you and I'll respect your decision, but I can't wait
forever. Hit me up when you're ready. For something
real.

That was the last communication Theo had with Sierra. He called her repeatedly, and she refused to answer. Theo went from being on top of the moon to feeling like the gunk at the bottom of a swamp. Maybe he was wrong. He thought they connected; he felt it with every fiber in his being. They didn't even have sex, and yet it was so powerful. That doesn't happen with superficial attraction. He knew that from his time with Kisha. They had six intense months together, but it was not love. Kisha still texted him. She even showed up at his job from time to time. Theo wasn't innocent. He did respond to the *U up* texts and sometimes he sent them. He knew it had to end. Sierra warned him about Kisha, but she was so fine; he fell hard for her. It was infatuation, but he didn't know it at the time. Kisha was not a bad person, but she was insecure and overly possessive.

Theo was an affectionate man and enjoyed spoiling any woman he was with, but he needed space and independence too. Being a good provider was important to him, along with his family. If a woman couldn't understand that he held his parents in high esteem and that they would be an active part of his life, then the relationship was dead before it bloomed. Kisha was not a person who could understand that. Her heart had been broken too many times before, by boyfriends, lovers, and her own family. Theo couldn't help her, though he tried. He hated getting the restraining order, but he feared for his mom and Sierra. Not seriously, but enough to take action. He never told them about the threats she made. Nothing transpired, so he didn't report her for violating the restraining order when she sent texts and showed up nearby. He didn't want to hurt Kisha. Theo still cared for her and hoped she had gotten some help.

Kisha, like most of the girls he dated, took issue with Sierra being his best friend. Sierra intimidated them. They were jealous or believed it was one too many people in the relationship. Either way, they didn't want Sierra around, but he couldn't imagine his life without her. It wasn't fair to the women he dated, and it was not fair to Sierra. He knew that.

Theo's heart belonged to Sierra. After all this time, he let himself believe it was finally happening. He expected he and Sierra and Jordan would be a family. Not right away. He knew Sierra was loyal to a fault, that's why she hadn't left Latavius earlier, not in jail or since he'd gotten out, even though their relationship was rocky. He knew because she confided in him. How could she not have felt the same thing that he did that night? She had to, but maybe she couldn't admit it.

Theo was keenly aware he was in love with Sierra and didn't know how to escape it. He didn't want to, but the truth was that Sierra had looked past him for years. Theo was always the guy Sierra could rely on. He was there whenever she needed him, but he never got the girl. How many boyfriends had he watched come and go? How many times did he serve as the crying shoulder? The dutiful best childhood friend. He needed more.

Sierra made her choice clear. She wanted Latavius, or so she said. Even if she didn't, she chose him, again. Theo refused to act out of desperation. He was a good man, and he deserved someone who wanted him in turn. He had yet to get any complaints in the bedroom and ooh the things he wanted to do with and to Sierra. He tried to clear his head from any romantic thoughts of the woman of his dreams. Theo volunteered to go on a work trip. There was a large marketing conference in Phoenix, and he had the chance to land new clients. It would be a welcomed distraction. He didn't know if Sierra would ever allow him in her life again. He already missed Jordan, but if Sierra truly wanted Latavius, then that's how it had to be. He realized he was no longer satisfied with being a fill-in. If he couldn't have Sierra completely, then he had to let her go. He prayed he wasn't giving up too soon. His heart was full, but he had to let go.

Theo's mom, Alicia, adored Sierra. She watched her grow up and saw how wonderful she and Theo vibed off of one another, like a hand in a glove. She would welcome Sierra as a daughter-in-law in a heartbeat. However, Alicia had grown tired of watching her son wait for a woman who was spoken for. His father, Frank, told Theo that he would have to let her go at some point. If it was real, if it was meant, it would happen in due time. Still, he implored his son not to give up, after all; it took Frank three years to even get Alicia to look at him. Theo packed his bags. A week's long trip, something that would have normally felt like a lifetime. Time away from the woman who owned his heart, was a necessary reprieve. He took the next flight out.

19

Bitter air froze the room over. Plastic hung over windows that didn't respect it. The wind entered the poorly insulated house with the force of an air conditioner. The men kept their coats on. No one desired to spend any appreciable amount of time there. In and out was the expectation. Latavius-highly agitated-refused to sit.

"This is some bullshit, man. Nobody said anything about coming by the spot. This house got heat on it. What the fuck this got to do with me looking out?" Latavius said to Dre and within earshot of Tremaine.

"Chill the fuck out, man. We just playing it safe. Shit, these cops out here like it's Halloween." Halloween was one of the most profitable days for Dre and his crew, but Valentine's day didn't disappoint. It all came with heavy policing. "Twan said he tappin' in, in a minute, so quit whining like a bitch."

"I'm doing this shit to square up with you, but I ain't ya' bitch. Your bitch at home."

Tremaine jumped in. *Damn! Muthafuckas always wanted to fight.*

"Don't get distracted. Let's get this business done and get the fuck outta here." Tremaine busied himself while they waited. He ran a Mecke test on the molly to determine how pure it was.

"Dammmnnn. That shit so blue it's almost black! The suburbs gone eat this shit up. Pure as fuck! I don't even need to try to sell it," Slim said giddily.

"As long as you don't cut it with no bullshit Vicodin or coke," Latavius said

"Oh, you back in the game now? I thought you was one and done," Dre challenged.

"Nah. But I know what the fuck I'm talking about. Greed will fuck you over every time." Latavius wouldn't admit he got a sense of excitement, looking at the drugs, being around what he knew best.

Tremaine was glad he got them refocused, "Ain't nobody cutting. The cocaine ain't for this."

"Tremaine, you talking like you did the dead drop. My pahtna risked his life bringing that *fire* in from Canada. But it's all about expanding. If you ain't selling to the suburban kids, you losing business."

Tremaine couldn't stand Dre. If it wasn't for his street reputation and money, he wouldn't be in this dump right now. But Latavius was too close to him. He had to see this through so he could disassociate with this motherfucker. He refused to go down with a snitch.

"I do right by my customers. Ain't nobody gotta worry about me cutting. I don't operate like that," Slim said defending his drug manufacturing skills. He took it personally, and these mo-fos needed to get the fuck out of his work area sooner than later. They were sniffing around too long, and he didn't know that muscle-bound punk telling him how to cut.

What the fuck was he doing there, anyway?

Dre's phone lit up, and he saw the unknown number calling his phone. "Yeah," Dre answered.

The caller on the other end wasn't heard by anyone else.

"A'ight. Bet." Dre ended the call.

Dre turned to Latavius and Tremaine. "He here. Let's get this shit right." He looked at Slim. "Go get the door, man. Make yourself useful."

Slim scurried to the door, embarrassed but too afraid to say anything.

"Latavius, don't you say shit. You just the muscle. And Tremaine don't give him shit until I verify this load. Don't hesitate to light these muthafuckers up if shit goes sideways. My boys on the street outside laying low, waiting just in case."

Latavius looked uncomfortable.

"What? Don't act like you don't know your way around a piece. You got the 9-millimeter I gave you and everybody know you carry a throwaway piece. Prison ain't made you soft. Let's get this package and get the fuck outta here."

***

I don't like to be kept waiting, she texted.

Marissa's expectations of Valentine's night had not panned out. Derek drove them to his cousin's house off Joy road. He promised it would be a quick drop off. Marissa didn't ask questions; she had zero interest in whatever business he was handling there. The Yukon Denali was warm and kept her in full comfort, but 20 minutes had passed, and her stomach was growling. She was texting Sierra about what could be her last date with Derek before her trip to Puerto

Rico. Marissa silently kicked herself for telling Sierra where she was. Her phone was blowing up now.

Sierra was nervous about the 48204-she lived there for a stint when Shandra was struggling hard. Marissa was quite aware of the dangers of Joy Road and Detroit's plethora of abandoned houses. It was like the city gave up on itself and part of the reason she needed to get away from there. There were two Detroits-one for the haves, and the rest were unappetizing leftovers for the have nots. Marissa lived in her share of foster homes on the east and west side, but she mostly lived in homes on the other side of 8-mile road, same as she did with her parents and Abuela. Marissa didn't feel guilty about being spoiled in the world of the haves by her admirers, but she loved her hometown, friends she had made, and it hurt her to see Detroit being forgotten, but she felt helpless to do anything about it. The city leaders committed to downtown's success, only. Beyond that, the rest of Detroit was on its own. Puerto Rico also had its struggles. She researched thoroughly, but she was ready for the change. Maybe it would be her fresh start.

Sea, I'm good. Derek said he'll be done in a few minutes. No worries, Marissa texted.

Now that Latavius had finally come home, Sierra had been more obsessive than ever. Marissa understood that Sierra was afraid that she might leave for good, but she thought Sierra should put her energy into her family. Instead, she was laser-focused on her friends, calling Marissa and Lane several times a day, to check-in or say hi. Sierra was a known texter, but recently she behaved like she just discovered the phone had a talk option. Marissa got a weird vibe from her bestie. Was she avoiding Latavius? She was sort of acting like a woman with a guilty conscience but Marissa believed it was more likely that Latavius cheated. She didn't trust that fool as far as she could see him, and she was nearsighted, so it wasn't very far. Latavius was too smooth. No man locked up all that time was perfect. No doubt he had bitches visiting him while he was in prison. Marissa wasn't new to the game, but Sierra was damn naïve, bless her heart.

Marissa's mind was racing in her boredom. She began thinking about Theo. Thank goodness she avoided that train wreck. Theo told her about his ex-girlfriend, Kisha. That girl was bat shit crazy. Theo was fine as fuck and she thought about hooking up with him, but she was over sex just for the sake of sex. Marissa needed more, and Theo couldn't deliver. He needed someone like Sierra.

"Enough was enough. This fool got me twisted," she said out loud. Marissa was a dime and would not be treated like some two-dollar ho. She was draped in red, looking like a whole snack. Marissa saw three men walk into the house. That was it. Derek had her twisted. *What the fuck was going on?*

If the party was inside, then it was better than being stuck outside. *She would tell Derek she had to use the bathroom and then they could take off,* she thought. Marissa turned the car off and walked to the door. Led by her Red Bottom boots, Marissa never made it inside.

Men ran out the front door, knocking her down in their fury, while shots sang a deafening ringing in her ears.

Pop! Pop! Pop!

Marissa Lopez was not as lucid as she was thirty seconds ago, but she knew she was at the wrong place at the most dangerous time. Her Abuela told her at a young age that a woman should always carry a .22. Marissa, laid out on the ground, instinctively reached for it.

20

Why did the phone number look familiar? Sierra silently questioned. She re-read the text.

Your man is mine. I know how he tastes, and he still wants me. He won't be yours much longer. Don't let V-day fool ya bitch. The text was followed up with a tongue, cucumber, and lips kiss emojis.

What in the world? Sierra thought. It had to be a wrong number; except she swore she recognized it. It was local with a 313-area code. *Hmm.* If the text was meant for her, then someone wanted her to think Latavius was cheating. Someone very lonely on Valentine's day. Latavius wouldn't cheat. He came back home. If he didn't want her, he would have stayed away.

Latavius was running behind. No doubt doing some last-minute Valentine's day shopping for their dinner. Sierra wasn't in the mood to go out and deal with crowds. They planned to have a quiet dinner in, a few chocolates, flowers, and she prayed for some off the wall love making. She was so pent up. Jordan was spending the night with his cousins at Charmaine's, so they were free to do whatever, wherever they wanted. A smile made its way across

Sierra's face and she checked her messages again. Still nothing from Latavius, just that suspicious text staring at her.

Who is this? No response. No read receipt. If the bitch didn't have the courage to reveal herself Sierra didn't think it was worth any more time in her head but as much as she tried, the message still re-played itself in her mind. She struggled in her fight against it.

She knew how she felt after her night with Theo, who she hadn't heard from in over a week, not even today. He always wished her a Happy Valentine's Day, but she couldn't blame him. She told him no, emphatically. Even if her heart continued to betray her, her focus had to be on her Valentine, Latavius. She was on her best behavior since that incident with Theo; much of her exemplary behavior was born from guilt. She hated to admit that, even to herself. Fear struck her in the heart. *Could Latavius be acting out of guilt?* Had she mistakenly placed her faith in him? Lane's accusation ran through her mind but she wasn't ready for that conversation. She didn't want to ruin their night, but she owed it to him to ask him about that weird text. It had to be nothing, and then they could get on with their lovemaking.

Her phone vibrated in her hand. She hoped for a second that it was Latavius, finally on his way. She wore her best negligee. It was hot pink with plenty of lace and fun openings. She was ready for her man. Sierra planned to tease him, so she covered herself up in her matching satin robe with pink house slippers, the kind with the ball of fur on top. Her pedicure was shiny with small heart accents. She knew she was stunning.

"Hi, Rita. Happy Valentine's Day." She wondered why her boss calling her. The store was closed.

"Happy Valentine's Day to you, Sierra. I'm so sorry to call you this late, but we have an emergency. I don't mean to ruin your night, but we had a break-in."

"What?! Oh my gosh."

"Yeah, it's a mess Sierra and we have two VIPs coming in tomorrow morning. We won't be fully prepared, but we can't leave it like this. The police just left. No witnesses. But it's a disaster. It's all hands on deck and I need you."

"Rita, I can't believe this, and I want to help. I do, but I'm waiting to hear back from Latavius-"

"Sierra, I really need you. I'll pay you double time. I need your eye. These mannequins must be styled by morning. I'll make it up somehow, I promise, but we need you. Please, Sierra."

Sierra felt a pit at the bottom of her gut. She worried about Marissa all day and now realized she didn't circle back with her and now someone had burglarized the store. *What kind of Valentine's Day was this?* It was worse than when Latavius was locked up. Something wasn't right, but she needed to step up. "Rita, of course. You've looked out for me more times than I can count."

"I'm so glad you said that. Your Lyft is outside."

***

Sierra failed to reach Marissa on her ride downtown. She was probably busy being spoiled by Derek. Sierra was jealous. She should be with

139

Latavius, who also wasn't responding to her texts. Charmaine never let her down. Sierra got to Facetime her #1 Valentine during the ride. Jordan was having a ton of fun with his cousins and didn't talk to her long, but he blew his mom a kiss through the phone and Sierra caught it on her cheek, leaving him rolling with laughter.

"Happy Valentine's Day, miss," the driver said as he pulled in front of the boutique.

"Thank you. Same to you." Sierra stepped down from the truck. She wore an old sweater and her house cleaning sweats and topped it off with her rain boots. There was more water than snow on the ground. Being stylish was not important right now. She had work to do. No way would she make it back at a decent time for Latavius, but she kept the negligee on, holding an ion of hope they could salvage their night. She had texted Latavius in the car and told him not to wait up and that she was okay but to text her when he arrived home.

The door didn't look broken. *Odd.* It was too dark to ascertain if windows were knocked out. Sierra walked through the open door. It was eerily quiet. *Where was everyone?*

"Rita," Sierra called out into the darkness. She found the light switch and flicked it to the upward position. Candles were everywhere, arranged on the floor and counter. Dim pink and red lights softly brightened the store in every direction, and danced off the flickering candles. Beautiful jazz tunes played through the boutique's sound system. There was a giant red heart of rose petals in the middle of the floor, and the man with the small box knelt inside of it.

"Happy Valentine's Day, baby. My heart doesn't beat without you. We're meant to love on each other, forever. I tried to stay angry with you, told myself I'm better off without you. I'm not. I'm crazy in love with you, Sea. I want to take you to the Ocean, fulfill all your dreams, baby. I will give you the world or die trying. Hold me to it. Please make me the happiest man on earth, Sea. Will you marry me?"

Her world was still. Sierra's hands were over her mouth. She dreamed of this moment as a young girl, dreamed of it with Latavius. The awe, love, and cartwheels her heart was doing showed through the tears that streamed down her cheeks.

"Theo, I love you too." The words flowed naturally off her lips. Her phone was ringing. She hit ignore, but it was her mother's ring tone. Her mom called a third time.

"Sea, is that a yes baby? My knee is getting sore down here," Theo said in jest.

"One second." She held her finger up, not holding back her joyful tears.

"Mom-"

"Sea, I've been trying to reach you. It's Marissa. She's been shot. She's in emergency surgery now."

"What?! Mom, no!"

"There's more Sea. Latavius was arrested. He's being held as a suspect."

Sierra's phone propelled from her hand, shattering into pieces over scattered blood-colored rose petals.

SPECIAL THANKS

I'd like to extend a sincere thank you to all the readers for taking time to read this novella. I hope you enjoyed Sierra's love story and tune in for the exciting conclusion! Please join the *Rhoades Readers* mailing list at www.rhoadeshousepublishing.com and be the first to learn out when, When Bae Came Home-Book Two will be released!

ABOUT THE AUTHOR

Syfari loves writing and bringing readers dramatic and thrilling stories! Syfari lives in Minneapolis with her husband and is the mother of two beautiful and socially-conscious people. Syfari enjoys reading, volunteering, and outdoor exercise when she isn't writing.

CPSIA information can be obtained
at www.ICGtesting.com
Printed in the USA
LVHW091757030921
696898LV00002B/79